CLICK

all my love goes out to

zoe
amanda
karen
dayna
christine
mom

new york city
portland, oregon

cʟɪcκ

a novel by kristopher young

edited by dayna crozier

cover art by jesse reno

cover design and
inside illustrations by kristopher young

another sky press
portland, oregon

a very limited handmade version of click was released in 2004
this is a first edition perfect bound published 2006
printed in the united states of america
ISBN 0-9776051-0-8

text and interior illustrations copyright kristopher young
contact kristopher at kristopher@anothersky.org

cover artwork copyright 2005 jesse reno
contact jesse at www.jessereno.com

cover and interior design by kristopher young

another sky press logo by steven spikoski
contact steven at www.stevenspikoski.com

click brought to you by
another sky press
p.o. box 14241
portland, oregon 97214
www.anothersky.org

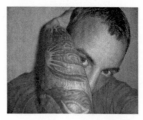

kristopher young lives in portland, oregon.
he writes.

jesse reno also lives in portland, oregon.
he paints.

Dear Reader,

Another Sky Press is a non-traditional publishing company located in Portland, Oregon. We operate under a progressive publishing and distribution paradigm that aims to directly benefit both audience and author.

The entire text of this novel is available for free online with a contribution requested but not required. We believe you, the reader, should be able to decide the value of art.

You may also purchase a trade paperback of this novel directly from our website at a sliding scale price that you set: the fixed third-party printing and shipping costs plus an optional contribution. This allows you to decide how much the author and publishing team earn by contributing at a level that is comfortable to you both ethically and financially. Removing middlemen such as bookstores and distributors (which can account for over half the cover price) allows us to ensure that significantly more money actually goes to the authors per book sale.

If you came across your copy of this book via a library, used book store or friend please consider contributing directly to the author at our website. This promotes passing along a book when you're finished with it (thus saving trees) while still allowing each reader to compensate the author if they choose.

Embrace the future. Support that which you love.

Thank you,
Another Sky Press
www.anothersky.org

psst! pass it on. ♻

rearrange and see it through
go where you think you want to go
do everything you were sent here for
fire at will if you hear that call
touch your hand to the wall at night

fugazi
promises

one must not put a loaded rifle on the
stage if no one is thinking of using it

anton chekhov
letter to a.s. lazarev-gruzinsky november 1, 1889

forgive me my dear if my
smile is cracked i've been
at war these 30 years past

billy childish
gentle men of gentle books know this

the best laid schemes o' mice
an' men gang aft agley

robert burns
to a mouse

for it matters not how small the
beginning may seem to be: what
is once well done is done forever

henry david thoreau
civil disobedience

contents

WBEGINNINGNEWBEGINNINGNEWBEGINNINGNE
EWBEGINNINGNEWBEGINNINGNEWBEGINNINGNE
EGINNINGNEWBEGINNINGNEWBEGINNINGNEWBEGIN
INGNEWBEGINNINGNEWBEGINNINGNEWBEGINNING
EWBEGINNINGNEWBEGINNINGNEWBEGINNINGNEW
GINN

do it, motherfucker.

do it! do it! what i need now is a wakeup call and what i've got is a siren blaring down on me, screaming six six six six six

six six six six six six six six six the word flashes by me, how many sixes does it take? counting sixes, i hear it morph into other words, i hear words i know i'm not thinking because i'm thinking six six six but all i can hear is sicks sicks sicks sicks cigs cigs cigs sex sex sex sex sex it's becoming something new again but i recognize it regardless of disguise. the chanting doesn't stop but somehow i don't lose count.

sixteen point six six percent repeating. one in six. i can visualize the insides of my finger tight against the trigger. i can feel every piece of me.

when the trigger clicks everything collapses, my mind races madly in every direction. the rush hits me so hard it sends me reeling. my eyes roll back into my head. i'm living independent of time. it's been abstracted to infinity and i'm in the all, the ever present now. no moment is over until i realize it's over—with enough like this one i could live forever. i'm awake. whole. new.

sixteen point six six repeating. i'm on the better edge of death; for once, i feel like the majority. i wonder if i'm looking maniacal or serene.

i aim at a wall and start pulling the trigger just to make sure the gun wouldn't have jammed. three clicks later it goes off, another climactic moment in a sea of brain fuck.

the gun rests in my hand, its energy expended. i let it drop to the bed with an impotent thud. there's a hole in the wall, a ringing in my ears that muffles the residual sixes echoing through my mind. no one complains, the cops never come. hell, dogs don't even bark.

i have my new beginning.

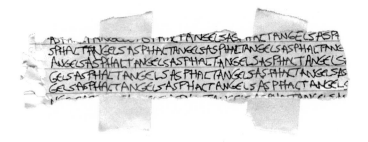

i'm down the stairs and out the door.

i'm shaking, explosive, i want to run up to strangers, grab them by their shoulders, tell them i've got it all figured out. i want to lay spread-eagle in the middle of the street making asphalt angels to the sound of blaring horns. i want to dance naked to the city's cacophony.

i can feel the ground seething beneath me, the life force pushing up through the pavement, the earth's teeming energy trying to break free of its prison. the evidence is everywhere, the small weed slipping through the cracks, the ant surfacing in search of a crumb, the rat clinging tightly to the gutter.

i don't remember ever feeling this way before. all the decay hits me as if it's new. this is what the world must look like to the innocent; infants, drooling at the mouth, see everything this way. every single moment is so heart-wrenchingly beautiful, every sideways glance the most perfect photograph.

survival gave me this. i could, and perhaps should, be dead but instead i'm alive and it's no longer a curse. i'm gifted with new clarity, an integral sense of self that was either misplaced or stolen long ago. my polarity has shifted, shining outward, no longer a collapsing star. and i'm smiling. people smile back as they pass me, and i'm thinking, if they only knew who i used to be. hell, who was i?

my job is a distant memory. i'm not even going to bother calling in sick. there's no way i could return to it, not after this. i'm no longer him. my savings will last for awhile— long enough, at least, that i don't have to concern myself with details now.

i've got nothing but time to burn so i walk the streets for hours heading nowhere in particular, taking it all in, gorging my senses, reveling in my skin. i'm avoiding habit and embracing new. random subways to random places, discovering cities within cities, turning only when traffic blocks my way.

the block of pavement directly in front of me details a history of abuse. cracks run through it like lightning descending from metallic clouds of grease pooled in the dark road sky. black trash bags are piled along the street, emanating the reek of discarded days. i feel the urge to rip them open, explore them, find some trace of myself in the rotting filth of others. i focus briefly on each piece of gum locked into the sidewalk, footnotes of the long and sordid history of the street chewed up, spit out and trampled. the trail leads to a cardboard box, its sides bashed and dented, scratched deep.

as i pass people on the streets, i'm looking into their eyes. they're overwhelming, too many eyes, lives behind them all. i'm stealing secrets, bathing in them. every person i see on the way reminds me of someone i know. it's in the lips, the nose, the way their jaw bone cuts across their face, but it's never in the eyes. one woman reminds me of a lost love, but much older, lost in time. her thick wrinkled skin hides her youth, but her eyes give her away.

an old man down the street, the perfect grandfather, gentle and kind. as i pass him i wave and say hi, and he returns the gesture, voice raspy like influenza. it's as if we've known each other for years. the small fence in front of his house has an intricate design, the masterpiece of some anonymous iron worker, intertwining crescent moons extending and wrapping themselves around their posts.

there's an open door, providing a split-second glimpse into another world. as i pass, i try to grab every detail, every nuance within. there's a rickety card table in the center of the room, covered in coffee stains and errant ashes, the tan paint peeling from its legs. four mismatched folding chairs surround the table, supporting four elderly men. they are dead serious, playing for their lives, not the cheap blue and red penny ante plastic chips strewn in front of them in lonely piles. the man facing the door looks up at me with his greedy eyes lost in his mottled italian face. he's always been sitting right there, his fat fingers gripping his greasy cards. it's the kind of game where whenever one of them passes away, another man who looks just the same fills his seat. i wonder if they ever bet on who will be next to leave their little game.

a tree trapped in concrete. it's a runt, skinny and bare, its smooth grayish brown bark marred by the raw remains of amputated branches. only the higher branches have persevered, bereft of leaves, flaring out in an electrical storm, defiantly declaring existence. as i pass i reach out my hand and run my fingers against its coarse bark.

above all of this, a flock of birds flies by, their liquid form in perfect function. they circle me twice, and then they're on their way, out of sight. beyond where they were there is a friendly dragon gliding the baby blue sky, two short ears wisping away from it, mouth gaping, fire breath escaping. the cloud grows into itself, breathing with the gentle breeze.

there's a dilapidated theater, long closed, that still emits the sickly scent of popcorn and rat poison. its front has given way to weather and graffiti, tired secrets buried under each other. next door is an OTB littered with men smoking cheap cigars and drinking from paper bags. the plate glass storefront allows a perfect view of the teeming masses inside, arthritic fists in the air, raging at the racing screens hanging from cold wood panel walls. they build to a crescendo, crossing their finish lines, bitter profanities cut with the occasional smile.

i see a parked car with its engine running so i take a deep breath and hold it. i'd rather suffocate than risk inhaling the dirty exhaust creeping along the sidewalk. i can feel it on me, scraping me, searching for a way in and then i'm through it, but still i'm holding my breath, it's another block before my lungs surrender to their need, purging themselves to suck in inviolate air. i feel pure.

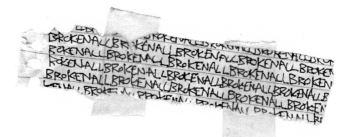

i'm standing on a corner when i see her. she's across the street, walking towards me. the sun itself is shining in deference to her, reflecting off her skin, glistening in her eyes, basking in her warmth. she's stepping out between two parked cars, looking straight at me, meeting my eyes.

i watch as the car smashes her. it isn't the movies, it's smacking a rag doll across the room, all broken bones as her face skids against asphalt, grinding into gore.

and then, just as suddenly, it's gone. the crumpled body, the pooling blood, the trail of pulped skin, the car. all gone, and there she is again, stepping out between the two cars. and i watch as the car smashes her, and it isn't the movies, it's smacking a rag doll across the room, all broken bones as her face skids against asphalt, grinding into gore.

and there she is again, stepping out between the two cars. and i watch in revulsion again, again, never ending, i watch and i want to scream but i'm locked in the same repetition as everything else.

and she's stepping out, only this time she must have caught a glimpse of the car out of the corner of her eye because she jumps back with this tiny little chirp of a scream as the car races past, oblivious to the future lost. the click was almost deafening to me, but no one else seemed to notice.

i don't know where i am, or rather, how i got here. my eyes are locked onto her, i could stare at her forever. i watch her head turn to the right, following the car as it rolls the corner stop sign, turning outside of sight and mind. she glances back to her left, nothing's coming this time. she crosses the street, her eyes fall back on me and light up as she catches me watching her. a crooked smile drifts across her face. i feel shy, nervous, so i close my eyes and when i reopen them she's disappeared, replaced by endless city.

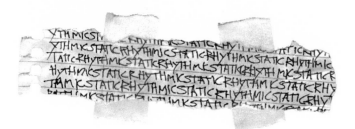

i'm impatient, i'm waiting. i'm pacing, excited, even though i'm not exactly sure what it is that i'm waiting for.

i'm in a small room with white walls, a low ceiling, and gray industrial carpeting. there is no furniture. no windows. a single door is the only way in or out and i'm cautiously eying it. i'm wondering what it means. music trickles over the intercom but i can't quite make out anything more than rhythmic static.

and then i remember what i'm waiting for. how could i forget? she's coming. and i'm happy. i'm not exactly sure who she is, but that's ok, because i know she'll have all the answers. i can't wait to see her. i can't wait to hold her in my arms.

the music is getting louder, a steady bass beat creeping out of the noise. as it builds the vibrations threaten to knock me down, i'm starting to feel nauseous. wait. the sound isn't music, it's someone knocking. it's her.

i open the door, but i can't quite make her out, she's steeped in shadows. i'm straining my eyes, for some reason i know i need to see her. i need to hold her. i step out of the room, going to her, but as soon as i do

pain. bright pain. confusion. and suddenly i know i am, and i wake to the sensation of the midday sun forcing itself upon me, raping my eyes. i rise to consciousness in a sort of free fall, light is pouring through the window, drowning me, blinding me and i don't know what to do so i wish it all away but nothing happens. i close my eyes but i'm still seeing red through the too thin flesh of my lids.

i hear whispering behind me, a voice slow and burning—*shut up... shut up... shut up...* i try to turn my head to see who's there no one should be there and i feel the fear creep into me *shut up* and i realize i'm still trying to turn my head but i can't, and the whispering continues *shut up* and i command myself goddammit turn your head but i can't, move your fucking arm but i can't. so i stop trying, close my eyes, relax focus center and then quick turn my head a quarter inch *shut up* before it locks into position again. i want to scream but then i break free and my head whips around and no one is there except silence. i'm already questioning whether i really heard any voice at all.

and so i'm left alone sprawled naked across my bed, searching for memories of who i used to be and who i am, briefly latching on to my quickly fading dreams. but i can't hold on and fragments of my waking life start to take their place. i try to piece them together, jamming them into an impatient jigsaw puzzle, trying to make sense of the conflicting rumors of my existence.

something is off. i'm electric, yet i'm winding down. i have a sinking feeling this is all just a symptom.

i'm standing here, eyes closed, fists clenched, trying to focus, pull it all back inside me. i can still see the path in front of me but my thoughts keep returning to that endless moment.

i relive her getting hit by that car like it was now. images of her destroyed body litter every thought. when i glance in the mirror, i see her eyes before my own take their place. i can reconstruct every detail about her, down to the green flecks like islands in her ocean blue eyes, down to the subtle imperfections in her skin, things i couldn't possibly have seen yet know are true.

it's a riddle, nagging at me. i don't understand what i saw, why i experienced it thousands of times over, why it didn't happen. i feel like i'm trying to solve a puzzle without any pieces.

this is not good. it's stealing my clarity, slurring the awe. i'm forgetting who i am and becoming someone i don't want to be. again. i can't let that happen. shouldn't being who i am come easily? why do i feel like it's a constant struggle?

i need to recapture what i'm losing. there is only one way this is going to resolve itself.

sixsixsixsixsixsixsixsixsixsixsixsix

as i pull the trigger the universe races away from me only to inject itself back into me in a heartbeat, exploding into my bloodstream, filling me, completing me. i'm alive, and i'm not sure what to make of it. i go out into the world and find things beautiful again.

this time, it's just a cup of coffee. i watch it fall and shatter, fall and shatter, fall and shatter, an ocean's worth or more. and then, as if it never happened, my reflexes are a bit faster, and i don't drop the cup, and i hear, or maybe feel, the click. i'm left holding the cup, so surprised at this new turn of events that i spill it all over myself anyway.

later, i'm sitting on a park bench losing myself in a book, imagining myself deep down in a well. thank you. the words repeat themselves inside my head, slowly coming into focus, and i feel myself rising to the surface, brought back to the here and now. thank you, she repeats, and when i look over at her, recognition shocks me into silence. she's sitting right up against me, close enough that i want to back away, but i'm already at the end of the bench. her smile is taking up half her face, but it still doesn't have anything on her eyes. oh there you are, she's saying, i wasn't sure where you were. thank you for saving my life.

this entire interaction is thoroughly out of my control. i'm trying to figure out her words. i string them together, repeat them silently to myself, and it dawns on me that she knows. somehow she knows i saved her. i'm wondering how she found me, was she locked in that moment too?

that guy over there, and she points off into the distance at no one in particular, that guy was following me. i think he was going to kill me. so i sat next to you, pretending i was with you. that made him go away. you saved me.

i look her over. she's short, petite, blond hair. cute. there's a fire in her, a way about her. what's your name, i ask, and she mumbles it under her breath like she's afraid to be known. i don't quite catch it but it doesn't feel right to ask her again.

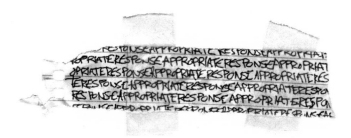

we spend the day together. not a moment seems forced, we have that rare and elusive connection. we're the children at the dawn of summer racing out of the house to play in the fields, holding hands through high grass exploring our new world. we're the mess of little hands racing haphazardly to complete the last few pieces of the puzzle, joining as one to put the last in place.

somehow it's already evening. the sun is setting, the sky darkening in purples and blues. we decide to get food and wander into a small joint, cozy and warm in its dim candlelight. i can't really afford the place but i don't let myself think about it. when my pasta comes i dig in, savoring the elegant sauce. she picks at hers briefly and then gently motions for the waiter. he comes over, she whispers into his ear and he takes her plate away. she's a pleasure to watch, so gentle in her actions, polite and graceful, so much so that i don't even bother asking why she sent it back.

afterwards, we grab a drink at a bar. we're sitting at a back booth, people are dancing to the music. we're cuddling together, watching everyone.

and suddenly, everything is different.

when i talk to her, she doesn't respond. she was pressing into me, whispering into my ear. smiling and joking, her soft laugh, her eyes and lips suggestive and alluring. but now her eyes are all over the room, flitting around in their sockets like buzzing flies. her face is still, pulled in on itself, as if she's suffering silently through some great agony and trying hard not to let it show.

i put my hand on her knee, but she pulls back from me, a frightened animal. her eyes are centered on my hands, her mouth quivering. she doesn't even know who i am. no, it's more than that, she's not even here, she's fallen deep into somewhere else, some place dark and scary.

i don't know what to do. i scan the room looking for some sort of clue.

my eyes come back to her, and now she's staring right back at me, her expression in bright contrast to how she looked just moments ago. she's glowing, absolutely glowing, biting her lower lip, a bundle of excitement. i love this place, she's saying, it's so cute. did you see the paintings? i think somebody famous must have done them because they're so beautiful. i bet you the artist is probably a millionaire and lives in some fancy mansion or has a cabin with a little pond.

are you ok, i ask, my voice low and tentative with the suspicion that one wrong move and she'll disappear on me again. of course i'm ok, silly! why wouldn't i be? you know what we should do tomorrow?! we should go to the zoo. they've got monkeys there, you know.

i'm not at a loss for words, there is simply no appropriate response. i find myself nodding my head, a coddling parent agreeing to a child's every whim. and i move my free hand to her lower back, gently massaging her and pulling her towards me. i don't hear her words anymore, but i'm still nodding my head.

sometimes moments scream out, cataclysmic. these are the crossroads, where the next footstep is of significant importance. i take her hand in mine and head back to my place.

we're lying in bed together, staring into each other. i can feel her presence against me, she is seeping from my skin. the voices in my head subsiding, the worries and random thoughts, replaced by the oneness of her eyes. staring into them, i feel complete. staring into them, i feel like this moment is forever.

i keep trying to convince myself that if i embrace love with my all the rest of the universe will click into place. it's not that nothing else will matter so much as everything else will make sense. this part of me wants to confess my love for her right here and now. but it's too soon so i hold onto my secret anyway, even though she probably already knows. it's a fucked up truth, and i don't want to scare her away with honesty. my heart aches from lessons learned.

breathe me in, she's saying, breathe in me. and i realize i've been holding my breath, and have been for some time. i press my lips gently against hers and inhale.

and then i hear her voice inside my head. it's ethereal, seductive and altogether subtle, a warm cadence of soft words flowing through me. and she's saying,

i promise i'll never leave you, together we can be everything. i'll fix everything broken inside of you.

i see something in you i forgot existed, she continues, but i know something's going on with you. i know you're having a hard time existing. but it's just an illusion, i'm right in front of you, and all you need to do is close your eyes and take a step forward and i'll be there. for you.

there's a silence, it's sitting there between us. and as it grows, it separates us. it's my move, but i just watched her reach out and pull us from the universe. she made it look so easy. how am i supposed to respond to something like that? and i'm slipping towards the end of the moment, falling, a thousand thoughts racing in combination so i just close my eyes and pull her towards me, accepting her in my embrace.

i can feel the universe shrinking. the infinity compressing into us, a tight ball of energy from which everything future will explode like another creation myth. maybe i should be scared of this, but i'm not. later that night, sleep comes more easily than it ever has.

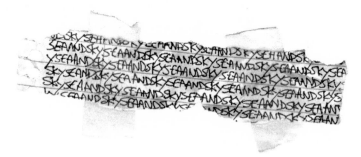

i'm standing in the center of a road in the middle of a desert, the asphalt dividing the earth between two opposing horizons. there's a cool breeze, the night sky lit by a calm moon, stars dancing gently in the sky like drowsy fireflies. along one side of the road run telephone poles placed at reassuring regularity, connecting people i cannot see.

my eyes come to rest on the nearest pole, and i watch as it smoothly transforms into totem, alive in carved wood, looking back at me with its long golem face. its mouth opens as if it's about to let forth a piercing scream but instead a single raven flies out and circles it once before coming to rest on the wires above. the totem closes its mouth and retreats into telephone pole obscurity. i study the raven expectantly, but it's just a raven, doing nothing in particular, paying me no mind.

i walk over to the shoulder of the road and sit cross-legged in the lazy dirt, my back braced against the pole. i notice a small stone laying directly in front of me. it's oval, about the size of a half dollar, polished in dark blues and greens swirled together like sea and sky. it feels warm in my hand, i'm holding it tight. i place the stone in my mouth and my moisture interacts with it, dissolving it. i swallow, feeling it work itself inside me.

the ground falls from beneath my feet, racing away from me. i'm above the desert, the raven, she's watching me, and then i'm beyond the earth. the stars surround me and sing to me in their distant language. i'm approaching the sun, i'm inside it, epicenter. i am of the sun—i feel its heat, but it doesn't burn.

i close my eyes, and when i reopen them i'm underwater. the currents wash over me, wrap themselves around me like a harem. thousands of tropical fish of every color pulsate in the water. they are watching me, circling me. they are in a perfect spherical formation, moving outwards, the sphere growing larger and the fish smaller until i can no longer see them. i float to the surface, exhale, inhale, and let the current bring me ashore. i fall asleep lying on my back in the warm, wet sand, the ocean lapping at my feet.

she's the essence of effortlessness. she's the princess of decay, her clothes worn into the ground, all the rips and tears sewn together until there's nothing left but her patchwork beauty. she cuts her own hair, it's always unkempt, jagged and chopped. she has this stunning smile, all teeth, that magnifies her beauty, but she tends to wield it at the most inappropriate times.

everything about her appearance just works. she's so good at being herself that i feel like maybe she can fix me, keep me from falling apart with thread and needles, scissors and glue.

she's brilliantly insane. her conversations are infinite tangents that rarely resolve themselves. her sentences are unrelated fragments lost at sea. her logic is intrinsically flawed, yet i constantly find myself amazed at her genius. i wonder if it's intentional, if she's just lashing out, fucking with the world, making shit up in a never ending verbal playground.

i find myself asking her random questions just to hear her trump my non sequiturs. i ask her what she thinks of electricity and find out it looks good. i ask her what she thinks of the mona lisa, and find out she likes the artist who painted her face, but not the one who did the background. i enjoy her for who she is and revel in her madness. from what i can gather, most people can't handle her. i'm enchanted by her reality, addicted to it.

she's contagious. i want to adopt her chaotic style, bombarding strangers with the twisted logic of nonsense and running circles around their attempts to understand me. would i be to them as she is to me? would it matter that it was on purpose? i would become her in an effort to make her what i want her to be.

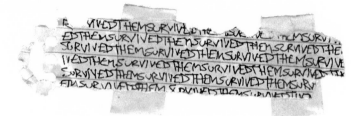

it's now, and i'm sitting on a bench in the park, waiting for her, watching the squirrels, watching people feed them. i'm not sure how long i've been here. and i sit and i watch it all go by; it all goes by and nothing i do can change or stop it. most of the people around me, walking by, walking their dogs, jogging, don't really hold my interest for more than a glance. if we could really sell our souls to the devil the world wouldn't be filled with so many ordinary people.

the man sitting on the bench across the way is busily scribbling in his notepad. he keeps glancing up at me, so i'm pretty sure he's sketching me. i don't know what to make of this. he doesn't know i'm on to him, i'm careful never to look at him directly. i'm feeling violated, i feel like getting up, moving somewhere, hiding. getting up, going over to him, screaming what gives you the right? getting up, peacefully asking to see his interpretation of me. in the end, i just downturn my head slightly to the right, giving him my best side. i sit there patiently, until i'm confident he's moved on to the old man sitting down from me. eventually both artist and subject are gone. i didn't notice them go. i've survived them both.

there's a squirrel maybe three feet in front of me. he's looking pretty brazen, so i toss him some of my unfinished bagel.

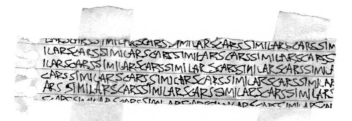

a man sits down across from me, some sort of weasel faced messiah, pockmarked with age, his deep sky eyes so kinetic that it's hard to look at him but harder to look away. i contemplate who he's going to save as we sit and stare at each other in some sort of silent battle or bond of friendship. i wonder what he's seeing in my eyes because i see worlds in his.

i go over to him and he nods his head to acknowledge me. his sleeves are rolled up, and there's a deep scar on his arm, purple, heavily keloided, surrounded by other, lesser scars. i can't keep my eyes off of them, even though staring makes me feel acutely uncomfortable. it's the same whenever i see someone deformed or disfigured, on the streets or in a shop or wherever. i feel guilty for looking, i feel guilty, maybe even more guilty, for averting my eyes, for shoving their existence into the recesses of invisibility. it's a no win situation, really, so i've made a habit of simply confronting people directly.

oh that, he says, is a surgery scar. see, i used to have this lump there, bigger than a marble, but flatter. it was there for years, and i'd run my fingers over it and wonder at it. i'd joke that it was my alien implant, you know, when that sort of thing comes up. i'd straight face it, never give a hint i was kidding. i was proud of it.

then one time, i went to the doctor for something or other and i asked him about it. he told me it was nothing to be concerned about. nothing to be concerned about? that got to me. i mean, it's better than hearing you've got a tumor, but fuck. i mean, i guess i didn't expect him to say it was an alien implant either. hell, i don't know what i wanted him to say.

point is, what he did say just wasn't working for me. so that night i decided to find out for myself. it didn't take long. cutting into my own flesh was... interesting, i could actually hear my skin splitting.

and then the man goes silent, as if he'd finished his story. i want to resist, i don't want to fall for his ploy. even so, i edge an inch closer to the man and, in an accidentally conspiratorial whisper, ask, so what did you find?

the man smiles, but just with the left side of his mouth, the heavy pockmarks echoing the dimple of his cheek. he reaches up to his neck, and pulls out a silver chain lost beneath his shirt. and he says, this, and displays the attached charm between his pinched fingers. and i'm not exactly sure what i'm looking at. it's porcelain yet metallic, hi-tech yet insectile, striking yet understated.

i look the man in the eyes, those blues searing into me, not sure how to respond. people just don't pull shit like that out of their bodies. then again, maybe he did, i wasn't there.

yeah, so i brought it to a jeweler, he continues, and had it mounted. the jeweler said he never saw anything like it, even offered to buy it from me. i didn't tell him what it was. i wasn't about to sell it, hell, it was my first, you know? my favorite too.

your first?

yeah. i've got quite the collection. sometimes i give them to friends. and with that, the man stands up, facing me, and lifts his shirt, and his entire chest and stomach are a scattershot of similar scars. i've got some more on my arms and legs too, they're kind of hard to keep up with.

i like you. most people look at me and can't see past the pain into the healing. they ask me: how could you do that to yourself? and well, it's who i am. a better question: how could i be who i'm not?

and then he's reaching for me, and i try to pull away but he has my hand in his, and he's pulling it towards him. here, feel, as he places my hand on his left hip, just above the line of his pants. his hand, still cupped above mine, pushes my fingers into his pliant skin. and i can feel it, something, under the skin. neither soft nor hard, but something is definitely there.

i found that one just last night, he says, as i pull my fingers away. i'm going to take it out soon, tonight probably, i don't like to leave them in for long. fuck knows what they're up to. and with that, he's got to be going, thanks for the conversation, maybe i'll see you around and he's walking away from me. i'm left sitting there, by myself on the bench, silent, fingering the small knot under the skin of my left forearm, rolling it under my fingers.

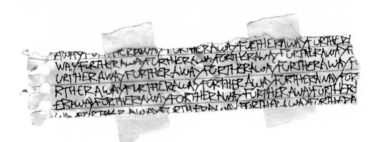

something breaks my trance. i look around, but nothing claims responsibility. however, i notice an old man sitting three benches down, armed with a paper bag breakfast. i wonder if he has anything interesting to say so i jump to my feet and cover the distance between us, and i'm sitting by his side, saying hello, introducing myself. he's all ramble and rant, words tumbling together. i was in them orchards, boy, as a boy, watching them grow tall like me but always in one place, see, and me and mine ate our fill, dammit, believe me when i tell you this it's good to eat your fill and they were there, and hah hah, yes, they were there and we all shared. i miss times like that not like now, i had to kill, boy, don't you see, all full of spit and lies and excuses they gave me a gun and said go kill that boy he's a threat to our way of life and i remember being there in that orchard and now it rains with blood.

i look at the old man in his old dirty fatigues and i ask him what it was like to kill a man. and he says to me, boy, he says, boy, to kill a man is to kill yourself.

there isn't much that i can add to that, after a while all the strangers' wisdom just sounds like rhetoric. so i nod to him, all politely with a have a good day sir. i turn around, and there she is, walking towards me. today her skin's looking a little dull and pallid, her eyes sunken, i think maybe she's suffering from a stomach virus.

we go into the subway station together. waiting, i notice someone lost an umbrella. further away, a doll's mangled remains. the train is coming, i can feel the breeze, the stagnant piss scented air circulating through the underground passages. we haven't even spoken yet.

on the train, i wonder if the guy standing in front of us even knows that he's covered in his own puke. there's a woman doing her nails, her plastic face molded in deep concentration. there's a fat child eating ice-cream out of a tub with his hands.

i look up at the advertised walls and it feels like it's all closing in on me. everywhere i look everything is bought and sold, and i don't understand why everyone isn't screaming, screaming in the train, screaming on the streets, rioting, ripping it all down, refusing the bullshit. i look around, and everyone's just sitting passively, maybe thinking this doesn't affect me, thinking this world exists for someone else. just like me. i keep my mouth shut, suppressing the outburst, pretending not to notice the three foot face of an airbrushed menace staring at me provokingly.

she taps me on the shoulder. i look at her, standing beside me, and she says, the people in this city, none of them like me, grinning broadly, only her eyes showing fear. i tell her not to think about it. but they're trying to kill me, she sneaks through her smile. i pretend not to hear her.

her skin smells of vanilla and french toast. my face is buried in her neck, i can feel her wool cap pushed up to my ear. we're holding each other, rocking gently back and forth in the chill night air. i can feel her shivering, we are one against the cold. i wish all moments were these moments. i wish for nothing else.

and then she pulls away, it's cold, can we go inside somewhere or something? i feel jilted by her callous indifference to what we were sharing, repulsed by the chasm. my anger growing, the overwhelming isolation, that impossible distance between everyone threatens my mind at every turn. every time i think i've found the solution i'm proved terribly wrong.

i just want there to be someone, somewhere who doesn't make me feel this way. apart. someone, somewhere, that doesn't feel a million miles away. someone i can trust. someone that isn't going to go away. someone who doesn't exist. i feel myself spinning into paranoia and i don't want to go there. it ruins everything beautiful, feeds off of love, turns it inside out so that i think it's hate and defensively hate back.

my eyes are empty as i respond to her, let's get some coffee. and i start walking, her faint footsteps falling in behind me. wait up, she laughs, catching up to me with a skipping hop.

we come across a little cafe and go inside. overly clean brick walls with comfortable pseudo-antique furniture. we sit down on a couch, and she leans up against me, her hand running along my inner thigh, but now i'm the one who can't recognize the moment. i feel claustrophobic at her touch. i want to pull away but i don't want to cause a scene. so many worlds, i'm always in the wrong one.

i excuse myself to the bathroom and busy myself reading the scrawled remnants of lost minds.

it's a shame our love is so mistimed.

we're lying in bed together. i'm looking at her, she's got this perfect form. her skin is stretched thin over her bones, her hips sticking out, her spine like sculpture, her neck the finest porcelain.

listen. you mean the world to me, i say to her. and that's why i need to walk away from this.

i say these words in a sort of desperation, not knowing if they're true, scared that they aren't.

the funny thing is, i really mean this bullshit, even as i watch the words fall out of my mouth like spilt wine staining tablecloth. i need to escape her gravitational force, pull away before she drives me mad.

what? what the fuck does that mean, her voice arched with half-formed anger as she turns over to look at me.

i don't know what it means, it means what i said. you mean the world to me. i need to walk away from this. which part don't you understand?

uh. all of it? you're a fucking asshole if you think you can get away with saying that as if it means something. she's staring me down, her eyes focused like razors, and i find myself studying my hands instead of looking at her.

yeah. you're right. it doesn't make any sense, but i don't know, maybe it isn't supposed to. i feel like this is a classic case of too much, too soon. i'm not sure if it's anything more than that. i like you a lot. we have a good time together. the sex is fantastic. but, i feel like i'm losing myself. i don't know who i am anymore. i feel transparent.

you don't look transparent. i can see you.

my face sort of falls apart and all that's left is a smile. her words dissolve my stern resolve, remind me of what drew me to her in the first place, so i pull her towards me, hugging her.

i'm sorry. i'm sorry.

that's ok, she says, returning the embrace. you didn't mean it anyway.

ANT REMINDER CONSTANT REMINDER CONSTANT REMINDER
ANT REMINDER CONSTANT REMINDER CONSTANT REMINDER
REMINDER CONSTANT REMINDER CONSTANT REMINDER CON
MINDER CONSTANT REMINDER CONSTANT REMINDER CONSTANT
R CONSTANT REMINDER CONSTANT REMINDER CONSTANT REM

much later, i need to get her out of my apartment so i suggest grabbing some food at the all night diner down the street. within a minute of getting our food she grabs the waiter's attention and barks, this tastes funny. he looks at her, and she's insistent, take it away, please. she hadn't even taken a single bite.

he looks at me, then down at my plate. maybe he's expecting me to send back my grilled cheese sandwich as well. i put my hand over it out of some sort of protective reflex, shaking my head no. after he goes, she grabs my pickle and takes a bite out of it. she's got that damn smile going full strength, so i don't really mind.

she watches me in silence as i finish eating, chug my lukewarm coffee. i tell her, i need to take care of some business so you better go home or something. she asks me, can't i just go back and sleep at your apartment, but i poker face her and say no, i don't think that's a good idea, i don't know when i'm going to be back. and then she's gone.

when i go to pay at the counter, there's a woman, maybe fifty or sixty years brooklyn, in line in front of me. after the guy behind the counter hands over her change, she fingers through the bills, saying something to the guy i can't quite make out. she passes him back a fiver, and he hands her another one apologetically, sorry ma'am, i wasn't thinking. after she's gone, i ask him what that was all about.

the bill, he says, had a rip. he says this matter of factly, he's used to dealing with people all day. i ask the guy for the five, giving him one of my own. i figure maybe i'll try to keep it, its insignificant tear a constant reminder.

i'm back in the night air, walking home, and then i'm in my bedroom again, i want to sleep but i can't stop remembering things i've forgotten, my memories injecting themselves rapid fire.

i remember this elderly couple, each riding some sort of electric cart, one behind the other. they were in the bike lane, putt putt putting along, about ten feet apart. both of them stared directly ahead, intently, their faces frozen in surreal expressions of fear as if the landscape was whipping by them in a frenzy. i will remember their faces even though they never saw mine.

i remember driving through an anonymous town late at night with an old girlfriend, one of those nameless places which may or may not have been on a map. it was winter and the trees were crystalline, magnificent sculptures with icicle leaves shimmering in the night air. the roads were empty, but we were stopped at a train crossing. i let my eyes trail along the tracks and jolted in my seat, hard. she asked me what was wrong, and it was everything i could do to point. her gaze followed the path of my outstretched arm, but she still wasn't sure what she was supposed to be looking at. look harder, i whispered under my breath, look harder. and then she gasped as the huge, monstrous train came into focus for her. it sat a mere fifteen feet from us, completely still in the darkness. it was masked against the black sky, watching us, towering over.

i remember hanging from a window twenty-odd stories up, a random point in the sky. we were laying on our backs, he and i, heads and chests out the window. a simple turn of the head produced waves of vertigo. we saw the sky as an ocean. the clouds sailed across it, we were above everything. we saw the blue sky end abruptly in the city haze, a perfect sky's horizon to the sea of blue. we looked at the street below, craning our heads backwards, backwards, ignoring the feeling of falling, knowing trusting we were secure. an intersection to the side of us was the deepest valley, trapping our eyes in a trick of perspective.

i can tell i'm getting tired, but i still can't fall asleep. my thoughts are starting to fragment. i've earned another sunrise laying here wide awake, listening to the liquid mechanical rumblings of the radiator. the constant hiss of steam that hasn't let up all night has left the apartment a furnace. the windows are open wide to compensate and the brisk early winter chill swirls with the rusty heat and caresses my skin.

random half asleep ramblings, i know i need to keep my mind quiet but i can't and it just pours forth incomplete thoughts all colliding into each other endlessly, i just want to sleep, i just want to close my eyes and forget, let my dreams resolve these issues and leave me newborn tomorrow morning. so i lay here watching lives go by, scripted disasters on the ceiling hidden in the shadows and counted in the cracks. all the mistakes i've made, a million car pile-up, and i'm coming up too fast, lost behind the dashboard, i feel the wheel in my hands but i can't make it turn.

and i don't know where i am, on a street or in my bed, slideshow vacation, it's all the same. i put my head in my hands, death grip trying to understand, and i scream, no this isn't really happening, it's all fake, it's all a sham, every day feels identical. i'm claustrophobic, trapped in artificiality, living in a box within a box within a box, and it's all made out of plastic, third rate manufactured reality. everything is paint on paper, i want to rip down my walls, rip down buildings, rip down people in search of something real. i want to rip my face off, fingernails screeching on skin like blackboard.

i sit up with a start, my back covered in sweat. i reach over to the nightstand, slide open the drawer, take out the revolver. i explore it, make sure everything's in order and put it on the pillow next to me, a gift to the tomorrow me. i can hear the city wake in the background, preparing itself for the day ahead, the steady beep beep beep of a truck reversing. i block it out, i'm counting sheep. but all i hear are sixes.

i'm in this room, and there is someone standing only a few feet away. there's a spark of recognition, it's a friend of mine. so i say hi, start to talk to her, but she's looking at me strangely. she doesn't recognize me. then i realize i'm mistaken, that she's not who i thought she was. yet as i fumble through my apologies to this stranger i realize i do know her, i was just mistaken at first as to who she was. but then she's not quite her either, and i realize her face is going through a litany of changes and i can never quite settle on who she is. she's staring at me as if i'm a madman, her eyes are asking, do i know you? and i want to say yes, but the name on the tip of my tongue is always two or three faces behind. no, i don't think i do, she's saying, my voice reduced to staccato bursts of near nonsense as i falter about my confusion.

i'm completely flustered. just then, a man with the most average face i've ever seen, dressed full tilt in an old-fashioned usher's suit, is telling me sir, would you please take a seat, sir, the show is about to start, sir. and i'm thinking, oh, ok, now i remember why i'm here.

it's a large theater, and the auditorium is crowded. i can hear the drone of simultaneous conversations interfering with my own thoughts. i can see movement out of the corner of my eyes but wherever i look there are only empty seats. soon enough, the lights dim and the screen goes white, but i can't make anything out. i can hear people laughing, ahhing at all the appropriate moments, but no matter how hard i concentrate i'm still staring at a blank screen wondering why i'm being left out. i'm getting tired, nodding off.

i don't remember falling asleep, but it must have happened.

i wake to her touch, her body pushing up against me. her arms are around me, her hands pushing into my back. my arms are around her too, so i pull our bodies tighter. we shift and move together in the darkness like two intertwining flames, separate yet not. i feel almost sexless, transcendent of physical need. we are sun and earth, two distant lovers finally afforded the chance to hold each other, with stars as audience to our union.

it occurs to me that my eyes are closed, so i open them. everything is dark. panic grips me, i need to see her, but no matter how many times i open my eyes they're still closed.

my mind is more alert now, questioning and trying to make sense of this strangeness. i feel myself drifting away from her and wish i had never tried to open my eyes in the first place. i catch my breath. for reasons unknown to me i am not allowed to see her. fine. i can still decide to be content in her warmth, in knowing she exists, in knowing we are one. but i'm still drifting.

i'm clawing at the moment, trying to pull myself back into it, trying to stay with her. but it's too late; i've figured it out—i'm dreaming. and with that my eyes open, and in the dim twilight i'm all alone, curled up in my bed.

i lay there in anger for a long time afterwards, unmoving, unsleeping. i could move if i wanted to, at least i think i could. why do i drive everything into the ground? if i could just stop thinking, just live in the moment, i might still be asleep. i might still be in her arms.

the dreams are always different but they're always the same. she's there and we're meeting for the first time, i've known her my entire life. we're meant to be, and we both know it. but i can't begin to describe her, i don't even know what she looks like. i'm not allowed to remember her face.

these dreams of her, of this faceless, nameless woman, of the fullness of what love could be destroy my waking relationships. nobody can compete with her, at least no one i've met. i'm not blaming them, i know it's my fault. i never quite let them in, i never give them the chance to fail me.

i notice the pistol lying on the pillow beside me. good morning. i pull the trigger, i survive again, and i feel a surge, a newness, but somehow it doesn't feel the same.

they should just kill everyone! everyone that doesn't have a car, kill them all!

i look up and the woman is shuffling towards me, ranting, looking directly at me. her face is so caked in makeup that her drunken eyes, the only real thing about her, end up looking even more plastic than everything else, guilty by association. they light up when she catches mine in hers, and now she's talking to me, she has her audience. the cars! they don't let you cross the street! her voice is haggard, strained. they have no respect for anyone, they'd be happier if we were all dead and out of their way!

she isn't turning her neck as she passes, but her eyes are locked to mine, rotating wildly off-center in their sockets. and finally she's past me, i'm out of her field of vision, and she's still going on about the cars, the cars, as her voice fades into the distance. i used to think it strange to hear people talking to themselves.

a morbidly obese pigeon takes a lethargic dive and lands a few feet in front of me. i'm only half paying attention to it, half watching as a car brakes hard and the driver honks at a pedestrian crossing the street.

a woman walks up and squats beside the pigeon, her unruly hair suggesting the morning after. her lipstick matches the kerchief around her neck, her sharp features could down a man with a glance. aware eyes peek out through her bangs, brutal and unforgiving, a promise of paradise under the constant threat of deep fault lines crashing to earthquake.

she reaches into her jacket pocket and pulls out some crumbs, sprinkling them in front of the pigeon. it pecks at one, drops it, and then proceeds to ignore the rest. the woman, looking a bit peeved at the lack of gratitude, stands up and continues on her way.

now i'm curious, so i edge up to the pigeon. he's full and old, the color of soot and pollution, with charcoal breast and dark gray wings. he seems removed from his surroundings, either oblivious or unconcerned. i sit down on the curb beside him, no more than a foot away, at first studying him, and then watching the traffic with him. he doesn't even so much as glance at me. i feel a strong kinship with this bird, but i don't know why. eventually he waddles away, slow but steady.

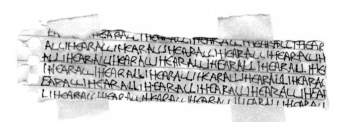

as i'm walking home, a cockroach races out from under some trash bags. it stops only a few feet in front of me, right in the center of the sidewalk. i squat down, my splayed fingers resting on the concrete for balance as i study it, lost in the intricate details. six finely barbed legs and two smooth antennae, body fat and bloated, rusty brown with a gentle hint of reddish gold.

and then some woman is edging around me, her movement startling the cockroach into a furious scurry. it races into the path of her step, and i'm holding my breath, i don't want to watch it die. and i feel death deep inside of me, constricting my heart as i watch her thick sole come crushing down on the cockroach, destroying it, its carcass crunched into the pavement.

i feel like i'm going to puke, and again i watch as her foot slaughters it, catastrophe, ignorance mangling innocence. again and again and again, over and over, i watch her annihilate it. and then i manage to shout, watch out, in a coarse half shriek, scaring her, she almost trips, she's stutter stepping, and the cockroach is through her gauntlet, safe in the shadows. she looks at me, and i know she's saying, asshole, but all i hear is the click.

it's hard to explain, but during the episodes of repetition, i don't exactly notice. i'm too busy regurgitating the same exact thoughts as if i'm part of the same broken record. it's not until the universe clicks back into place and life continues like normal, trudging along second by second, minute by minute, that i feel it. it's like that jolt when i'm falling asleep somewhere i shouldn't and i jump an inch in my seat.

it becomes obvious to me that i've been stuck looping the last few seconds for a small eternity, that i'd sucked every last bit of life out of it, the marrow from the bone. and after it's over, once the universe is back in working order, i look around to see if anyone else noticed the strange glitch in time, if anyone else saw what didn't really happen. no one ever does.

it's like there's some kind of mistake, some simple mistake, and the universe is righting itself. and i'm the only witness.

i have a working theory. maybe, just maybe, my mind keeps rejecting the now that is being forced upon me until reality itself mutates, until it becomes something i'm willing to let happen. and only then does the universe click into place. she was there, broken and dead and ruined for all time until i denied time, until i took it all back and sucked it all in and remade it. i changed the now and made it mine. but... it's hard to actually believe this to be the case—it feels too solipsistic.

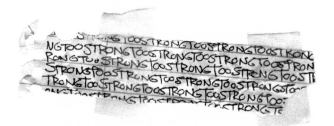

your eyes are too strong. what? i said, your eyes are too strong, she repeats. you should maybe keep them closed or else people won't want to talk to you. and i'm thinking, well, what if i don't want people to talk to me? and a hat. yes, a hat. that's what you need.

and so i find myself accompanying her to a thrift store, but by the time we get there she's long forgotten about the hat. once inside, she's trying on everything, going through the racks with abandon. right now she's wearing a shirt made for some giant, she looks like a child trying on her father's clothes. she's got on a prom dress. a long striped scarf. a faded suede jacket.

i'm not going to get anything, she's saying to me, and the rampage is over. and we're out the door and down the street before i realize she's got on a different outfit than before. she's changed completely, her old self left scattered on the floor of the shop, lost amid other unwanted secondhand dreams.

i notice a gaggle of tourists rambling toward us. there's a woman snapping pictures recklessly, so i raise my arms reflexively, blocking my face from her prying lens. i'm the accidental subject of photos, living in the background. the guy jumping for cover, trying not to be abstracted by technology, frozen in time.

i realize we're at a bus stop; i'm not really waiting for the bus, but she seems content so i decide to stand with her. we're there for maybe five minutes when a blind woman taps her way to the stop. i'm watching well-dressed vultures, one after the other, eating her desiccated remains, feeding their egos. is everything ok, miss? do you need help? one woman asks her what bus she's waiting for and then assures her that she's at the right stop.

the bus comes, and she lets go of my hand, saying to me, perfect timing, as she jumps on board. i get on too, deciding i'd prefer to be someplace else. on the bus, i discover everyone likes to stare at blind people. it's the perfect form of voyeurism, you can never get caught. the woman gets off a few stops later. at least four people tell her to watch her step.

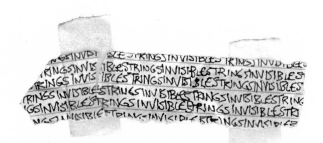

we're sitting at a bar, holding hands. i'm eavesdropping on the conversation next to me. some woman is telling her friend about how she just went on prozac. it frightens me how open people are about this sort of thing. drug history as pedigree. she's laundry listing her issues, her vanilla flavored neuroses. i'm wondering what she used to be like, before.

eventually, they get up and leave the bar and i shift my attention back to her. her thumb is rolling in the palm of my hand. she looks beautiful in the soft lighting, eyes dancing with the candlelight.

she's saying, everything had these invisible strings attached to them, and i could never let the strings get tangled. if i picked up this glass, for example, i'd need to make sure it was put back exactly as it was. if i turned to talk to someone, i'd have to be careful not to get trapped by the string.

and i'm thinking, that sounds pretty cool. i can almost see the strings myself now that she's got me concentrating on them. i wonder if she knows something nobody else knows. her perspective would certainly go far in explaining so much of the confusion in the world, the blind billions leaving everything wrapped up in nasty little knots.

she's telling me, i turned to prozac to get things sorted out for myself, but i stopped taking it a few years ago. she adds cheerfully, but i don't see the strings anymore, anyway. my whiskey scented curiosity gets the best of me, and i can't help asking, what if you see them again someday and realize what a tangled web you've weaved? she looks at me a bit funny, and excuses herself to the bathroom.

when she comes back, it's like the conversation never happened. she sits down and she's talking about what we're going to do tomorrow. every conversation i have with her started well before i even got there and finishes without me even knowing it.

and we're in my bed. i wonder if maybe she's got tapeworm. as much as i want to ignore it, it's obvious something's definitely off about her. she can feel so different. it's in her eyes. and it's more than that. i can't help thinking she looks a little ill. but i can't put my finger on it, every time i see her, she seems to have a brand new disease.

43

i look over at her and she's a million miles away. this makes me sad, this wall between us, but i'd be lying if i said it wasn't always there. even with it, i can see all the hurt in her, all the loss, all the pain. and i just want to reach out and touch her but she wouldn't understand. i do it anyway, taking her hand and giving it a soft squeeze. she looks up from her thoughts and asks, what the fuck was that? nothing, i respond, i just felt like holding your hand. even the best intentions can be a violation.

she's saying to me, we have nothing in common. and i bite my tongue, thinking, well, who does?

i don't know what to make of you, she says. you're so sweet and real and when i walk beside you i can feel your spirit ten feet tall, but... something inside you, something's off. i'm not really sure what it is but i know you've buried something inside you and i'm scared to find out what it is.

i'm taken aback by the clarity of her words and once again see her for her. i want to start over. i think back to the words she once stole my heart with, and i find myself saying to her, you know all the badness in the world? all the hurt and fear and sadness? maybe together we can create our own little place, one where all those things don't exist, where we trust each other and hold each other and never take looking into each other's eyes for granted, one where the entire universe melts away and leaves us standing in fields of us, warm and full and together, where we share ourselves and shed our skins and crumble our walls and never let ourselves destroy what is beautiful, never let ourselves forget what love is.

44

i'm not sure if i believe the words i'm saying or if i'm just spouting bullshit. as they leave my mouth they already feel brittle and frail, another failed ideal, empty of the purity of her own distant promises to me, victim to my lack of innocence. it's like i believe in just a little bit of everything, only to find those little bits cancelling each other out, irreconcilable, then negated. so i lay there naked beside her, and i look into her eyes and i don't say anything more, i don't commit to words. i just run my hand down the small of her back and feel my cock pulse in the heat of us.

i guess what i'm saying, she continues (as if i hadn't even said a thing), is that you scare the fuck out of me. it's your way, i don't know how else to put it, but i feel like you exist in some other universe than most people, that you could manipulate me with ease if you wanted to. and i run my fingers through her hair, a light smile on my lips, my eyes say, no, no, i would never do that to you and i wrap my arms around her and pull her tight. she reacts like an animal when she feels me press up against her stomach and she rises above me and grinds me inside her.

she's asleep in my bed, and i'm sitting in the other room. i can't fall asleep with her there. that's not really fair, though, since i probably wouldn't be able to sleep anyway.

besides, i'm still thinking about her string theory. i'm analyzing my actions, digging at my personality, searching for any similar quirks. i can come up with a few bad habits, but nothing half as interesting as hers.

i grab an empty notebook from a pile in the corner of the room, a pencil from a long ignored drawer. i start writing. at first the repetition is boring and rote, but i can tell i'm on to something. soon the lines come easy, long division until my hand is cramping in pain. i can't let myself stop—it's always just one more page, one in six goes on and on.

i force myself deeper and deeper into it. it's become a part of me. an urge, an itch. it's never quite right, just one more six, i need to do it just perfectly, just so. and i can't stop until i do. my head is starting to hurt.

it's time for the test. i stop writing. i have the pencil pressed against the page, keeping it there, but not letting myself move on to the next six. my mind is screaming at me in mutiny, finish it, finish what you started. i need to close my eyes. i start counting to myself, anything to subdue the overwhelming desire to complete the ritual. i'm in the thousands, jaw clenched, by the time the urge subsides. victory.

and with it, peace washes over me; it's not as intense as when i survive the gun, but it's still a liberation, a release. but more than that—a sense of accomplishment.

46

i stare at the number i'm creating. i'm going to need more notebooks. i wonder how long i'll be able to beat the odds. statistically speaking, i've only got so much life left in me.

i wake to her shaking me, c'mon to bed, silly, what are you doing out here? her form is shadowed in the dim city light creeping in from the windows. she's wearing panties and nothing else. following her back into my bedroom seems like the best idea in the world.

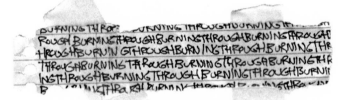

i'm completing notebooks at an alarming pace; piles of them, all brimming with sixes, threaten to take over my apartment. right now i'm burning through one, only a few pages left. i've got it perfected, line after line of identical sixes packed so tight against themselves as to be nearly unrecognizable.

i get on the subway and have to put my notebook away. i can't keep it as neat and orderly as i have to when everything around me is rattling.

but now when i'm not writing, i'm shaking. i fidget and twitch, anything to unleash the coarse energy coiled thick within me. it's a problem; sitting on the subway, i catch my knee jumping up and down rat-a-tat-tat, my reflection in the opposite window with jaw grinding heavily, chewing rocks. people are beginning to stare; to combat the unwanted attention, i try to contain myself, redirect the energy into little secrets, rolling my tongue across the insides of my teeth or tapping my thumb against my fingers.

it doesn't matter who i really am. all that matters is how i present myself. what i look like and what i say. that's all people will ever know. i sink deeper into my seat.

my eyes are tired, and i keep nodding off. every time i blink there's a new person across the car from me. i catch them all covertly staring at me, but not one returns my smile.

as soon as i get off the subway, i sit down and pull out a notebook. it feels good, but as my last six falls on the bottom right of the back cover, i decide this notebook will be my last. i have a new idea.

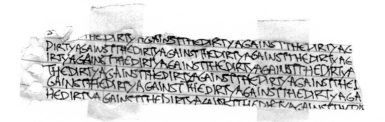

my walls are filling with calculation. i'm standing on a footstool in the corner of my bedroom. i'm on my tip toes, stretching up, my arm heavy holding its own weight, my wrist aching. i'm working on the first row of the third wall—this is the hardest line of them all, my hand tight against the ceiling.

i keep my writing tiny, tight, exact. each digit excruciatingly formed, the black ink crisp and sharp against the dirty white walls. i measure my pace carefully, giving each six time to dry so as not to smear it. this must be perfect.

i stand back and view my progress and i can feel their power. all those sixes, thousands of them, stare right back at me.

my creation sits dormant under the flashing lights, ignorant to the wailing alarms interrupting the thin night air. they're getting closer, steady bursts of machine gun fire followed by hollow screams. and i'm thinking, if i only had one more day. but instead i'm the castrated frankenstein, never getting to see the results of my labor open its eyes, never knowing if my life's work would have come to fruition. i kiss it goodbye, rub my hand lovingly across its cold cheek, and then i'm through the escape hatch, down into the sewers. my path is lit by flickering strobe lights placed every hundred feet or so. this makes the journey through the long tunnel feel eerily disconnected, someone's low budget version of hyperspace.

the tunnel reeks of refuse, rank shit, decaying animals. i can see myself in each burst of light stuttering in slow motion.

there's water in the sewer, thick sludge, getting deeper. but it's not slowing me down, if anything, i'm faster, gliding over it. but soon, it's so deep that i can no longer run upright without banging my head into the ceiling, so i dive into it instead. i'm surprised by how clear the water is. the smell is gone, and i'm wondering why i didn't think of this sooner. i swim until the tunnel comes to an end and find a ladder leading to the surface.

i emerge in the middle of an empty road, and i'm not exactly sure what i'm supposed to do until a taxi turns the corner. i hail it and wait patiently as it pulls up alongside me. i feel a momentary recognition of the driver, but i can't place him and the feeling quickly passes. i'm inside the cab and rattling off directions to my apartment. the driver turns around, and with a dapper smile, says, i know where you need to be.

and then we're racing through the streets, reckless, and the driver is laughing maniacally as i cower in the back seat. i try the doors, but they're locked, the windows won't roll down. the back compartment of the taxi is filling with the smoke of cheap incense. i'm gagging, choking, i can't breathe, the scent is smothering like car exhaust, i can feel my throat dry with dehydration, taste blood as each cough cuts into me. and then, finally, i pass out.

i'm in the center of a gray sky, holding onto a rope. nothing is visible in any direction. i ascend the rope a hundred feet or so, and then realize it would have been easier to go down instead. and then i'm thinking, fuck it, so i just let go. as i fall, i close my eyes. when i reopen them, i'm back in the cab.

but now there's a woman beside me. we're stopped, and the driver turns around, get out. get out, get out, get out. his words have the low bass growl of a demon in heat. the two of us get out, and then the cab is gone even though we haven't paid the fare. i look around and realize we're at the hideout. we go in, and there are maybe five others milling about. everyone's panicked, irrational.

a man stands up and states, i'm going to go kill myself, and promptly walks into the next room and closes the door behind him. no one seems to notice except me, so i'm yelling at them, are you just going to sit here and let this happen? the woman from the cab is whispering to me, don't worry, i know him, he's just fooling around. he doesn't mean it. and i'm screaming, no no no no no no, don't you fucking get it? and i'm up, to the door, opening it.

the door frames a picture-perfect moment, only it looks like someone took a squeegee to it. everything is completely still, yet blurred slightly to the side. and in the center of it all, the man is standing there, a sawed off shotgun in his mouth. and as soon as i grasp the totality of what i'm seeing, he's pulling the trigger, blood and brains vomiting from the back of his head in semi-translucent arcs. everything still has that sense of blur.

the first thing i think is, whoa, i just saw someone blow his fucking head off, you can't even pay to see something like that. i quickly push that thought away, bury it, and i'm turning as the blood starts to pour out of his nose and mouth, turning before the body even hits the ground, screaming at the rest of them, you bastards, you're just sitting there, you let this happen. and the woman, with a glimmer to her eyes, is saying, well, what the fuck do i know? besides, you're the only one who could have stopped him. this is all your fault, really.

before i can respond, the wall to my left collapses with a muffled explosion. and through the dust, i can make out a monstrosity. it's my creation, but it's no longer mine. it's deformed, mutated. it has somehow transformed into a mechanically organic nightmare, a strange octopus-like creature walking on long tentacles. and as its laser eyes slice through me all i can think is, my creation! it's alive!

paranoid schizophrenic is a pretty heavy phrase, yet for whatever reason it still slides right off the tongue. paranoid schizophrenic. schizoid. schizo. psychosis. that fucking lunatic. you fucking psycho.

'this condition is characterized by preoccupation with systematic delusions.'

grandeur.
persecution.
reference.

as in: god told me my infant son was the source of all evil.

one of my uncles was that crazy. seriously cracked. deep, dark, family secret. i remember him as: kind, caring... a big brother i never had. i practically lived with him—he lived with my grandparents and i stayed there while my father was at work. i was about seven when he died in a car accident. i remember crying a lot. i remember not going to the funeral. i remember missing him.

all those childhood memories completely fucked by one word: infanticide. my father found the mutilated remains. i didn't learn about any of this until two decades later when i was in my mid-twenties, even though at the time it was ripe for prime-time television. history unraveling when you least expect it.

my aunt on my mother's side was paranoid schizophrenic too—i remember visiting her in the hospital every once in a while growing up. but she didn't kill any babies, or at least that secret was better kept.

heredity is an interesting word that i'd rather not think about. sometimes i wonder if my conception was more of a game of genetic russian roulette than anything else.

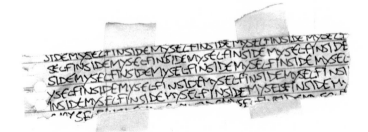

my walls are covered in solution, my apartment devoured by sixes. i'm laying naked in my bed, looking up at them as they weave in and out of the cracks in the paint like little ants whenever headlights pass the windows. in daylight, they are strong and imposing; they give the apartment character. i've never really painted or done any serious interior decorating; usually my walls are white and empty. i prefer this.

everything is covered, not just the walls and ceilings, but the insides of closets. the top edges of doorways. behind the refrigerator. underneath the face plates of light switches. everything. everywhere.

home should be where you are comfortable, and now i feel as if i'm inside myself. it feels right. it's inarguably mine.

every morning, i'm waking up to the sixes. i can no longer go without, starting off the day with the gun has become routine. there are a lot of holes in the wall.

pulling the trigger never gets any easier. knowing the odds are in my favor doesn't mean much when i have a revolver jammed in my mouth. each time, i'm that much more definite that the chamber has come to rest in the fatal position. each time, i face my reckoning. afterwards, i feel the rush but it never lasts quite as long as the time before. i'm scared.

statistically speaking, i can't live forever. so why am i? morning ritual, sixteen point six six percent repeating, i'm beating the odds into submission, the numbers melting into each other and sliding down the wall where my gore should rightfully be. it doesn't make any sense, i don't know why i'm still alive, all i know is that i can't stop. it's beyond need, it is everything i have been, everything i am, and everything i will ever be. i've lost track of why i even do it. i guess it's for all the obvious reasons, whatever those are.

i'm keeping track of the bullet's position each time, measuring how close i came to death in sixteen point six six degree increments. maybe, if i live long enough, i'll do some statistical analysis. i keep a note to myself taped to the wall next to my bed (it took me a while to decide what tense to write it in.) it reads: i'm not depressed, i just want to see if i can do it.

i survived again this morning, and now the phone's ringing and i don't want to get it. i pick it up anyway, thinking maybe it'll be some salesperson i can give the runaround to. sir, i'd like to take a moment of your time to tell you about our product, it's quite amazing, it will make your life worth living. oh really, i respond, please do. and on and on, for as long as i can string it out, until his voice is strained and cracked and he finally hangs up on the most inquisitive customer in the world.

but none of this happens, it's her, and i'm thinking fuck fuck fuck what was i thinking, i should have let the machine get it. and she wants to hang out, and for some reason i agree to meet her in an hour. i'm not sure if i can deal with her today.

i stand, walk into the bathroom to take a piss. it feels warm inside my cock and sounds cold against the porcelain. i don't flush.

i look into the mirror above the sink and see myself old. why is it that every morning feels like staggering out of a ten year coma? i give myself my best angle in the mirror, running my hand through my stubble. i can taste yesterday's food in my mouth, mixed under the foul taste of morning.

my teeth hurt, and i flick my tongue against the cracked tooth in the rear of my mouth. i don't know how many years have passed since that happened. many. the tooth is at a slight angle, the victim of the pressure of long removed wisdom teeth. food gets trapped there and i can often feel it warm and fester. i consider yanking the tooth out myself, but i know i won't. sometimes i feel like that tooth is an anchor in my life. no matter where i am or what's become of me, i'll still have that dull ache. it's a constant, letting everything else i experience define itself as now.

it takes me a while to get out of my apartment, suspicious that i'm forgetting something. but there's nothing to forget, i have my keys, wallet. i grab a notebook and a pencil but i still can't quite brush the feeling away. i walk up and down the stairs of my building a few times, hoping the ritual will somehow solve the riddle. but no, and finally fuck it, i'm going and i'm out the front door and to the subway station. i just miss a train. damn it. i should have brought a book, and then the import of that thought registers and damn it again, two-time loser. it's not my day. frickin' phone.

i'm on the subway when i catch another man sketching me, his rhythmic glances giving him away. he looks european, a rugged face drawn in thick dark lines. i'm prepared for him this time. i open my notebook to a fresh page and then we're at each other. it doesn't take long for him to figure out what i'm doing, i have his rhythm down and our mirrored glances crash into each other time and time again. i start with his eyes, his fat blue eyes deep in their sockets. his raised cheekbones and full lips. my line work is heavy and ugly, dirty. two stops later he's gone. but it's too late, i have him, we've traded ourselves.

there's a reeking mess of a man stumbling down the subway aisle, scratching, mumbling to himself. i recognize him, i've seen him on an irregular basis for the past few years. he's the most wretched case of humanity, it makes me angry at the world to see someone this way. it's an uneasy disgust i'd rather aim at the people dropping enough cash on a single meal to feed dozens. we allowed

this to happen to this man, and i don't forgive myself for
that. we are always and only our lowest form. he wanders
in front of me, stops, and i'm holding my breath until my
face turns blue to avoid the harsh scent of shit. the train
pulls up to my stop and i'm out.

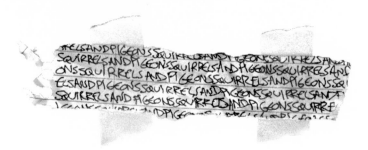

i'm standing here, waiting for her, watching two kids
walking together, singing. one's got a yo-yo in his hand,
the other, a stick. their voices come into focus, they're
wailing at the top of their lungs, row row row your boat.
both drop their toys to start chasing squirrels and pigeons,
yelling gleefully, cheering each other on like heroes.

i see a bike messenger cutting through the street, he's
twenty-something, skinny, ink running down both arms.
suddenly i can't breathe. there's no longer any air.

i'm watching as he juts left to avoid a car and crashes into
one of the kids. he's thrown from the bike. the kid is flung
down hard, smacking his head against the ground. and
everything loops. i'm watching it happen again. again.
again.

and then, finally, he juts right instead of left, directly into
oncoming traffic. his head goes through the windshield. i
feel everything click.

there are shouts in the air. i can't move, i'm fixed in place, and suddenly there's too much air and i'm hyperventilating.

i fall into myself, losing track of everything for a few seconds or minutes and then the chaos around me pulls me back, reminds me of what just occurred. a crowd has gathered, medics on the scene.

and i remember the loop, and how everything still went wrong. if i have any sort of control over them, i caused him to get hit. or maybe i've completely lost it. i try hard to stop thinking about it. i want to leave. but i'm still waiting for her.

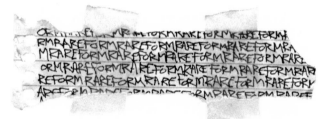

when i finally see her approaching, she's looking sort of malnourished. i can almost smell the bulimia, her teeth starting to look rotten, worn down by bile and stomach acids. this girl needs professional help. soon. i smile, she smiles back, and i give her a big sweeping hug, spinning her around, but i quickly put her down, worried maybe i might crush her brittle bones.

after what just happened i decide i should confide in her. but not here. i ask her where we're heading, but she dodges the question, already half into a conversation. she's in rare form, i can't make sense of anything she's saying. i can tell she's speaking english, but that's about it. i nod my head to the beat of her confusion, and i'm thinking get me the fuck out of here. so much for confiding in her. then she's not talking anymore, and it's almost as if her eyes change color. she starts up again but this time i can understand what she's saying.

it's hard to trust anyone, you know, when everyone you've ever loved has tried to kill you, her smile so wide you can see gums. she sent me away, you know, told people i was paranoid schizophrenic. you don't think i'm crazy, do you? i never really thought about it, i say. i don't say to her, but yes, you probably are. she had me put away for six whole months, and people forced me to take drugs every day. i almost died, they were trying to kill me. they made me take so many drugs, now i feel totally fucked up, i think maybe they made me crazy. you don't think i'm crazy, do you, she asks, wide eyes full of delight.

i shake my head no, mouthing the word yes, and she's saying good, i don't think i'm crazy, either, although i get scared sometimes that i am. i hate them, i really do, and they're the ones who tried to kill me in the first place. i raise my eyebrows inquisitively, resigned to the fact that there is no way out of this conversation. and it's all pouring out of her, she poisoned me and then claimed i tried to kill myself. but i didn't, i swear, all i had to eat was some soup she made for me. and then i passed out, and they found tranqs in my system. do you know what it's like knowing your mom tried to kill you, but not knowing why? i mean, that's enough to make anyone paranoid, right?

and i'm thinking poor, crazy girl, she's lost and confused, and i decide to reach out, maybe try to help her. my gut tells me she's delusional, and even if she's not, that's such a horrible way to go through life, thinking thoughts like that.

so i take her face in my hands, cupping her chin, tracing the contours of her face, my fingertips coming to rest just below her eyes. look me in the eyes, and she does. and i'm staring her down, forcing myself into her, and i'm asking did you take those pills. no, she asserts. this is important, i say, did you take those pills. no, her eyes betraying her, all i took were some zinc pills my mom had in the bathroom.

i take my hands from her face but don't break my stare. tell me about the pills, i demand, softly, imperatively. they were just some vitamins in the medicine cabinet, nothing. they weren't nothing, i insist. they were pills that you took the night you ended up in the hospital for almost killing yourself. don't you see? your mom had nothing to do with it, you took those pills yourself. i back off a bit, letting the nature of my words sink into her.

i give her a way out, maybe those pills were in the wrong bottle, i theorize, maybe the original bottle was hard to open, so your mom put them in a different bottle, not thinking anyone else would take them. maybe the whole incident was nothing but an accident, no, i'm sure of it, because, really, that makes so much more sense than your mom trying to kill you, right? she pauses tentatively before responding, it does? so i burn into her eyes and state plainly in a knowing, soothing voice, yes, it does. and i taste victory, her eyes wash over as she's jolted into a new reality. you're right, she's saying softly, i never thought of that.

we're still standing exactly where we met, but she's making me feel uncomfortable, so i start walking away from her. i don't look back. i feel like i violated her, but i'm not sure i had any choice. we are just our memories after all, and usually, we're misremembering everything anyhow. what's one more incorrect recollection? she catches up to me and grabs onto my hand, smiling madly.

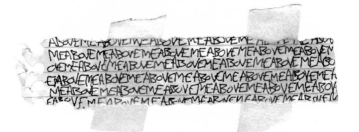

the first memory i have didn't really happen. i remember being in a white room, second hand furniture strewn all around, a bedraggled oriental carpet hiding the worn wooden floors. my father was above me to my left. my mother was above me to my right. and they were arguing in words i couldn't comprehend. i was screaming, or maybe just thinking no no no no no no. i think i knew she was leaving but i couldn't understand why. when i think back to this moment, it feels like someone's scraping my mind from my skull, dislodging it.

but it didn't happen. or at least, i don't think it happened. my mother left without a word. she disappeared with a guy she had only met a few days before. she wasn't well.

she wasn't exactly stable. when i was much older, my father gave me a collection of letters she had sent to me over the course of the following year or two. i was too young for them then. i think i still am, but sometimes i read them anyway. i rarely think it's a good idea at the time, and never do afterwards.

who am i when i can't trust my own past? i'm never sure what memories are true, and i have no idea of what i've forgotten, so all i'm left with are these conflicting voices of past mes, screaming for attention—this is who i was, so this is who i should be! but they never agree, an infinite number of voices colliding in my head making the singular me that exists at this very moment... what? a self-induced fabrication, a vulture, always circling, hungering over the truths i once knew but have long since forgotten.

later, she's leaving my apartment again. where is she going? i have no idea where she lives. the more i think about it the more i realize i don't know much about her at all. where she was born. what she does for a living. everything is coming up blank. usually details like that seem so extraneous to me as to be pointless, so i never bother to ask. but right now, she's about to blink out of existence if i don't do something. i need to know more.

i get dressed as quickly as i can and i'm out the door. as long as i can make it to the subway station before the next train comes to take her away i'll be fine. it's dark outside, misting. there's a cold thick breeze in the air, a heavy night. i feel invisible under its weight.

i edge down the station stairwell carefully, trying not to make a sound. she's at the far end, staring at the ground in front of her, not paying attention to anything or anyone. we didn't exactly part on the best terms. that's mostly my fault.

she's standing on the edge of the platform, wavering unsteadily. she looks like she's about to fall forward into the abyss, her erratic stance is making me nervous. i want to run up to her and pull her to safety. but i just stand there, half hidden behind tiled pillar, as i feel the rush of air and hear the approaching rumble of the next train. i'm still watching as she seems to come to attention, taking two steps back to safety. i saw other things happen. i feel nauseated with images of horrors that weren't, ragged amputations, writhing decapitations.

once she steps on board, i sprint down and jump into the car next to hers, jamming myself between the closing doors. i position myself where i can view her through the small windows in the doors between us. her face is wrought with tears. i want to go over to her and hold her. but i can't.

it's that lonely time between passed out drunks and half asleep workers, so the train is mostly empty. there's only one other person sharing this car with me. he's middle aged, slouched over on himself, practically falling to the floor. three chins and working on a fourth, his breaths loud and congested, snores that aren't quite snores. i can't tell if he's drunk or just exhausted, but i'd bet on the latter. i wonder if he's someone's father. i wonder if he's got someone waiting for him somewhere.

many stops later, we transfer to a train waiting across the platform. i watch the man, still sleeping, as we leave him far behind. it's only a few more stops before we transfer again. i don't think i've even been on this train before. i pass the time watching the graffiti blur by. she's nodding off.

when we finally get off the train, she's still in another world. we're the only two on the platform, so i'm careful as i shadow her movements. up and out, i feel like we're in a different city. as we walk, me tailing a block behind her, shops turn to residential turn to warehouse and factory. she stops in front of a large beast of a building, a converted warehouse, maybe, and fumbles for her keys.

so now i know. i turn around and head home.

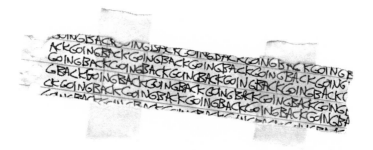

i'm pretty sure i survived again this morning, but i can't exactly remember. when the phone rings, i answer it but don't recognize the voice. i'm not sure how they got the number. a bus ride, and now i'm in a hospital. i haven't seen my family in a long time.

my grandfather lays dying. third stroke, this one is the end. he's weak. he reminds me of a corpse. he was a strong man, but now his arms are thin, mottled flesh hanging from the bones. his once imposing physique has given way to skeleton. his mouth hangs open. his glazed blue eyes are larger than i remember them, but they seem lost, he never really focuses on anything. i barely recognize him yet see myself, this is time laid out before me, this is me in fifty odd years.

he sort of mumbles and i can't make out anything he's saying. my aunt is telling me she heard him say applesauce earlier, so they made sure he got some.

my aunt is still talking, are you going to need some time alone with him? the question implies i'm supposed to answer yes. i answer no anyway. i don't know what to make of any of this. i have memories of my grandfather and they are not this. i'd rather not be here. i do not want to see him like this. i don't need to make my peace. i don't feel guilty.

it seems so simple. he is dying, as am i. he will die and so will i. everything is as it should be.

i'm distant, so far away. i know i'm sad. i mean, i must be. but i don't actually feel anything. i'm not grieving the way everyone else seems to be, and it makes me wonder if something is wrong with me, or if they're just faking it.

i sit down on the bed next to him, taking his limp hand in mine. he's shaking badly, his hand jumping arhythmically. i run my other hand through his sparse white hair. i lean in close and tell him i love him. i have nothing else to say, i'd rather sit in silence. i'd rather listen to him, even if it's only mumbled applesauce.

i'm looking at him, and all the war stories he told me throughout my youth come rushing back. my grandfather, like many grandfathers, enlisted in the days following pearl harbor. he was stationed on a destroyer in the atlantic. i've heard most of his stories countless times. i've never heard any of them enough.

my favorite:

my grandfather doesn't take guff from anyone, never has. one day, this bully started giving him shit. most guys were scared of this guy because it was well known that he had been a professional boxer. my grandfather didn't back down.

words were exchanged and a challenge was made; before he knew it my grandfather found himself in the ship's makeshift boxing ring with this guy bearing down on him.

when i was a kid, i always wanted him to tell me how he wiped the floor with this guy. but he didn't. instead, he was pummeled in that ring. he lost, but he refused to go down, he took punch after punch until he was a bloody mess.

the next morning, my grandfather felt beaten and embarrassed. but when he entered the mess hall everyone began to cheer, hurrahs and proud slaps on his back.

a few minutes later the boxer walked in, his proud victory smirk trumped by a single black eye. sometimes that's all it takes. his smirk melted as the room filled with jeers and heckles.

that's my grandfather. he'd fight anyone he had to, he'd stand his ground, he'd survive whatever challenges were put in front of him.

his ship was eventually sunk by the japanese. he was one of the last left on board, they'd run out of life preservers and he survived by jumping overboard and swimming out to a mattress floating in the ocean. he then paddled his way to a nearby ship despite receiving heavy internal injuries from the shock waves of bombs exploding in the water.

and now he lies bedridden, shaking from parkinsons, addled with stroke, losing his mind to alzheimers. and people think they're doing him a favor by plugging him into machines that keep him breathing an extra day or week or month.

the family is gathered around him. and he's mumbling again, but this time i can hear his words like they were carved into the air. he's saying, it's time, it's time to go.

only some of us hear what he is saying.

as we're being herded out of the room i want to rip the fucking clock off the wall.

later, lying in bed, i'm visualizing myself inside a hospital room. eyes closed, i can see the sterility and wires and machines, i can hear the buzz of electricity, the footsteps of nurses, the uneasy congestion of the dying. i cannot be with him, but i'll share his fate. it seems the least i can do. i'm not going back.

i'm running through a forest, and i can hear the rustle of pursuit. i'm full force ahead, galloping, cold with fear, dodging the trees as they approach me. branches are clawing for my eyes. i'm stumbling haphazardly but i know i can never stop. i'm barefoot running in mud. it's getting deeper, bogging me down until i'm rooted in place. but the trees are still racing by me faster than ever, as if the earth is still turning without me, leaving me behind.

i concentrate on freeing myself from the mud, i need to escape, i need to run, but when i look down there is no mud at all. i'm standing on puke green tiles, my ankles shackled. i'm thinking, this makes perfect sense, no wonder i couldn't move. the trees are gone, replaced by tall men with long arms, smocked and masked. i'm the center of attention, basked in sterile light. the air is filled with a low rumbling chant that i can't quite figure out, and i wonder if it's coming from beneath those masks or from behind their hazy crimson eyes.

the men approach me, hold me. one removes the shackles, and then they're lifting me, carrying me, placing me on a metallic operating table. i want to ask them what they're doing, tell them there's nothing wrong with me, they've made some sort of mistake. but i can't open my mouth and i briefly wonder if i even have one. they pull my arms out to the sides, forcefully, and i raise my head just enough to see wires and tubes rise out of the table like robotic snakes, and they strike at me, piercing my wrists, restraining me to the table. my legs are similarly immobilized, my ankles crossed, held down by metal and plastic.

i look around but i can't see the men anymore. i'm alone in a bright white room, it smells of disinfectant. i'm hoping someone will come to rescue me, but then i notice that the room has no doors or windows. there's a whir of machinery, and i watch as a large machine rises from the ground beside the table. it's almost comical in its retro-science fiction, the year three thousand by way of nineteen fifty. i'm still trying to figure out what the device is trying to be when a small beam of red light emits from it, splitting open my side. i can smell my flesh burning. and then it's done and over, and the machine sinks back into the floor.

i'm in pain, and i can't keep my eyes off the long incision up my side, it's pulsating as if alive. it gapes open, and i watch in horror as my organs float out of it one by one, hovering in the air above me. i keep thinking, i need those, i need those. and then i notice that i'm not held down anymore, i'm rising, i'm swimming in the air, and begin grabbing for my innards. they're fish in the ocean and i'm the shark, devouring them one by one, gorging on myself.

something's definitely wrong with you, she's saying. you don't make much sense.

i feel like i've had this conversation before. so i ask her, what do you mean? and she's saying, well, for one, you don't make much sense. and something's definitely wrong with you. i can tell.

didn't she just say that? i'm not sure enough to reply. and she's still talking, we hang out, and we have such a good time together, and we fuck so good... but i feel like you hate me. you don't want me around. you never want me around and you're just screwing me because you've got nothing better to do.

no, i enjoy being with you. but even as i'm saying it, i know it isn't true. it's more that when she's not around i miss her and i want her and i love her. and when she is around, i hate her... i watch myself become a monster to her and i despise myself for it and and i despise her for making me feel that way. i want her away.

really and truly, she asks? and i don't know how to respond, because i want to soothe her but i also have an overwhelming urge to kick her out of my apartment, to be done with her once and for all. really and truly, i respond.

you're so sweet, she's saying, and i don't really know what she's talking about, i don't know how she arrives at her conclusions. her hand wanders down my stomach, between my legs. and then it's her mouth, wet and good. before long, we're doing it again. i don't really notice, my mind is on other things.

i'm not really sure it's art, but it's definitely a gallery, wide and spacious, high white walls dwarfing the prim and proper guests. everyone seems overly dressed, everyone has drink in hand. except me. i'm standing in the center, watching.

the soft laughter of the polite listener surrounds me, breaks through the dull drone of overheard words. pithy comments full of ingenuous appreciation. people giving the most useless advice to one another. rehashed proverbs spoken as if they're genius. television quotes dropping flat like microwave dinners.

the occasional gem—i hear a woman scoff, you know life's bad when you can find yourself in a pop song.

after a while, i start shaking. i'm not sure if it's noticeable or not. call it social anxiety, call it hating everyone around me. not a real hate, i save that for special occasions, but close enough. it's not that i have any ill will towards these people, it's just that the gap between us all makes me feel very, very alone.

and then i remember i'm with her. mission: need to find her, need to get out of here. go go go.

the place isn't that big, and i find her in the back. people are looking at her. it only takes half a second to realize something's terribly wrong with her, something i don't understand. i feel my own issues wash away, this is bigger than me. she's spitting. spitting everywhere. people are staring. she looks crazy, feral, possessed. i hear a man comment, she's probably epileptic.

i grab at her shoulders, look her in the eyes, but she's not there. she doesn't recognize me. she's saying, i see you looking at my eyes. i know you want to eat them. you're a rapist and a murderer. you want to take me home and fuck me. i know who you are, you're going to kill me. i know it. and then her face goes into a quick convulsion as if she sucked on an invisible lemon, and she spits at the ground. it's more going through the motions than anything else—her mouth is dry, her spittle barely mist.

i break free from her damning words. and as i'm stumbling backwards, she starts screaming fuck fuck fuck fuck fuck at a portrait on the wall. the woman within stares back in a frozen passion.

people are moving towards us, they want to stop her, to shut her up but they don't know what to do. i can almost hear them thinking, isn't somebody supposed to have these situations under control?

but i just turn, and push my way through the audience, knocking into them, drinks and ice spilling across hardwood floor in a post-modern splatter. i can still hear her, fuck fuck fuck fuck fuck. insanity as performance art. i'm gone.

i already know i'm going to call her. i'm much better at losing people through death than through life. death i can grasp. i can get my head around it, it seems natural and innately necessary.

i'm tortured by thoughts of those i was once close to who are now lost to me, a chasm deeper than death between us. sometimes i feel as if each time i lose someone in this way, another chunk of my heart becomes necrotic. i should be coughing up congealed blood by now.

we want to believe our words of devotion, even as we feel ourselves falling away from them. even as the arguments reach fever pitch and we tear holes into each other, two

74

frightened animals trying to escape the same tiny little cage.

how many feigned smiles? how many strained promises? *i will always remember you. i will always love you. we will be fine.*

if i could do anything, i think i'd want to apologize to those that mattered most. i'd want this apology to be eloquent. i'd want to feel the forgiveness of the universe rustle through me like a lover's hand through ruffled hair. but, of course, i can't find the words.

i can't find the words to say to her either. maybe it's too late to save her. and me, for that matter.

i'm standing on a street corner, waiting, when i see two guys collide into one another. it was an accident, neither were watching where they were going. they're both pretty big guys. very big, actually. one of the guys is wearing a baseball cap, and he's patting himself down, making sure he's all there. the other is wearing the uniform of some delivery service, and without a pause he's yelling, what the fuck, man, watch where you're fucking going. baseball cap snaps back, fuck off, you blind? and then it's water pouring from a faucet:

you tellin' me to fuck off, man?

who you think you fucking talking to?

step, motherfucker.

and then the guy with the baseball cap changes gears, starts to back off, and he's saying, i don't got no beef with you. but uniform isn't letting up, motherfucker, step to this, bitch. baseball cap is still on the retreat, but uniform is screaming you fucking pussy ass bitch. and as baseball cap snaps you can feel it in the air. i watch as he pulls back and surges forward in a crashing wave, cracking his fist into uniform's face. uniform is thrown down to one knee, and i'm thinking, damn, front row seat.

and then baseball cap simply turns around and walks away, and as uniform rises to his feet i'm thinking, oh fuck, i already know how this is going to end. uniform is reaching into his pocket, and i want to scream watch out, watch your fucking back, but i can't seem to make my mouth work. and uniform yells motherfucker and trots towards the other guy.

baseball cap is turning and i watch as he gets knifed in the neck, blood spurting into the air. he's turning and i watch as he deflects the knife with his forearm. he's turning, and i watch as he jumps back to safety. he's turning, and his stomach is opened up like a burst water balloon. he's turning, and the blade slashes across his mouth, leaving a gaping smile. again and again, every variation, until i feel as if i've seen every possible thing that could ever hope to happen. and it's a rabbit punch, knife puncturing heart, that finally clicks with actuality. and everything is moving forward again and the blood is spouting out from his chest in orgasmic bursts.

i'm shaking. something's really wrong with me. i want to rip my eyes out, i'm seeing too much. i'm nauseous, as if i've been spinning circles arms out wide. i don't understand, the loop was so different from all the others... not one alternative, but the many. i don't want to do this anymore. i want off the ride.

i have no choice and there's no time to think about it anyway. baseball cap is in shock, clutching his blood soaked chest, stumbling away. there's a small crowd of captivated pedestrians, heads turning silently, following him. uniform is looking at his blade, sort of mystified by it. but he snaps out of it quickly and takes a few steps and stabs the guy twice more in the stomach to finish him off.

and now the crowd is all shouts and screams. uniform just walks away, even stooping to pick up a discarded piece of newspaper to wipe clean his blade. no one stops him. there's a woman's voice echoing in my mind, strangulated in horror, gasping, screaming, you're not supposed to do that! but obviously, he was.

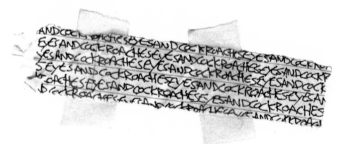

i have the sudden urge for tea, so i grab the kettle and put some water on. i go into the living room to wait. the walls are that aged white, discolored with time and smoke and the smudged black fingerprints of waist high children. there's a ragged oriental rug stretched across most of the floor, framed on all four sides by dark oak. there's only one piece of furniture in the room, a small green recliner. it's facing away from me. a child's handprint, etched in paint, mars its back.

i sit down in the chair to find the springs are all broken. there's a doorway (with no door) in front of me. the next room is swarming with darkness, but i think i can just make out someone staring back at me. i find this odd; i thought i was alone. i strain my eyes and now i'm sure someone is there. we're watching each other, the dimly lit eyes even with my own. whoever it is isn't moving. shivers run through me as i consider that i might be sharing an uncomfortable silence with a corpse. i'm rooted in my seat, all i can do is stare harder. it's hurting my head.

whoever it is still isn't moving. and now the darkness of the other room is seeping into this one like smoke, reaching in, stealing the light in sudden, jerky motions. slow tendrils of it are crawling along the walls, the floor, the ceiling. there's an urgency, if the darkness reaches me before i figure out who the person in the other room is, i'll suffer his fate. i'm not sure why i know this, but i do, i feel it in the pit of my stomach. i close my eyes and concentrate. deep breaths. a mantra: when i open my eyes, i will see him. when i open my eyes, i will see him. when i open my eyes, i will see him.

and when i open my eyes, i do see him. it's a face i recognize, but drawn tight and anorexic, with worms for eyes and cockroaches half burrowed into skin. a mouth gaping open, filled with maggots. small things crawling under the flesh, tiny little bulges pushing around the cheeks and forehead. he sits on a throne of green, majestic, a king of death and despair. and though his face is destroyed, he's so obviously me. and then i realize that it isn't a doorway i'm looking through, it's a mirror. and i try to scream, but my mouth is stuffed with maggots. i can feel them falling down my neck and chin, creeping down my throat. they taste of shit.

a shrill whistle splits through the room, the water boils in the kitchen. i jump to my feet and go fix the tea. i stand by the mug, staring into it as it brews. the way the tea blackens the water reminds me of something, but i'm not quite sure what. after a few minutes, i take a sip. the tea tastes musty and old, but it's still better than the odd taste in my mouth. it's too hot, it's burning my mouth, but i gulp it down anyway. as i near the bottom, i start to get queasy. something's definitely wrong with this tea. and then i notice the teabag isn't a teabag. it's a dead mouse. instead of retching i'm just standing there, staring at it.

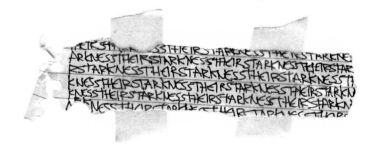

the phone rings. i never understand why i bother to answer it.

my uncle is dead, defeated by deep-rooted alcoholism and the ravages of aids. everybody knew his demise would be soon, nobody expected today would be the day. suicide was ruled out—this gives the family a sense of relief. i'm not so sure it wasn't, but i keep my suspicions to myself. he drowned in his tub. or fell. or something. he had quit drinking only a few days before—my father said he had the dt's really bad, shaking violently, his withered legs struggling to hold him up, threatening to give out with every step.

the last time i saw him he was so very frail, skin and bones. he was gaunt, the face of aids, sunken eyes peering out of thinly fleshed skull, his hair long and unkempt. the drunken poet, he lived in poverty and alcohol. even so, his strength was apparent, his features only that much more beautiful for their starkness. he'd lasted a decade longer than the doctors had told him, and he did this despite refusals to take medication, despite living heatless winters to fuel his addiction.

describing him feels like describing a lost cause, someone who fell through the cracks. but i'm not—he was one of the strongest souls i've ever known. a man i'm proud to be related to. an artist and musician to put others to shame. a hard temper hiding the kindest heart.

like his father before him, he was full of stories. he told me how he'd always wanted to write them down before it was too late, but he always ended up throwing out every page as soon as he finished it. i can relate; i feel the same way every time i nod off to sleep.

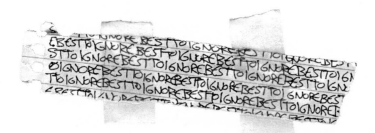

i've got my hand around her throat, gripping too tight, and her eyes are locked on mine, questioning. my fingers push into her mouth, and she's sucking them. i'm running them through her hair. i'm ripping my nails down her back, drawing blood as she gasps in pleasure. i... don't really know what i'm doing when everything clicks. something. she seems happy enough, so it couldn't have been too awful.

it feels like i'm fucking her forever. i feel ill with the things i've seen myself do to her. the possibilities. but she doesn't know any of that. she only knows about what actually happened, even if i'm not exactly sure what that was. i can't confide in her, i can't confide in anyone.

later, she's sitting on my bed, naked and satisfied, covered in me. i ask her to leave. both of us are still breathing hard, sweat streaming down my forehead. as she dresses she's staring at me, she's got this look in her eyes that i try my best to ignore. i get out of bed and open the door for her. she walks through, turns around, and she's standing just outside my apartment, facing me, still with that look in her eyes. i close the door. a few minutes later i realize i didn't even say goodbye... but it's too late, she's long gone.

i curl up on my bed and suffer. how could i do that to her? how could i treat her like that? she loves me. and i love her. maybe. in a broken sort of way. i want to go find her, hold her, let her know i'm sorry, that i didn't know what i was doing. that i finally understand, everything's been made clear to me, i'll never fail her again. but this is tempered with the knowledge that i don't want her to come back. ever. i want her to be finished with me because if we keep going like this i'm just going to make the same mistakes. i want so many different things that i don't know what i want.

i feel paralyzed. so i roar, guttural, and it comes from so deep it feels as if i'm trying to eviscerate myself. and it isn't stopping so i'm forcing my face into a pillow, muffling it, suffocating it. i'm pummeling the mattress with my fists until my knuckles are raw and bleeding. but nothing is solved and i'm still full of conflict. i take the gun out, preparing it for the morning. i make a silent wish that it's for the last time. but it probably isn't.

i find myself thinking about how i am to her, careless and unforgiving. i promise the world and give nothing of myself, a liar and a thief. and the whole time, she's so kind with that never ending smile, so sweet and i take it and i use it and i litter the ground with her sex. and even though i know i'm being hard on myself, critical, there's truth in it as well.

i won't let myself care about her. or possibly, the more i care about her the worse i treat her. maybe it's me trying to warn her, don't get close to me, run, get out, get out. but calling them warnings is as false as everything else, because it's me acting in this way that is the problem in the first place. if i wasn't trying to get her to hate me, she'd have no reason to.

and the memories keep pouring forth in a waterfall, accompanied by these searing arcs of sadness that race through me, and suddenly i feel too human, and i feel the food digesting in my stomach and feel naked and disgusting every flaw magnified and i raise my hands to cover my eyes but it's futile because it's all inside my head but i can't stop it and i can't stop feeling like a demon because now all i can remember are the times i was mean or cruel to past loves.

i remember screaming, destroying, fists clenched by my side, face red, eyes fierce, hatred pouring out of me. and it's only worse that i loved them with all that venom, because secretly i know how close i had been to smashing them, breaking their pretty faces. i know how hard it was not to cross that line, how deeply i cared about them even as i brought it all down around us, but all they knew was my anger. i'm so scared of the violence buried inside of me. i'm so scared i don't know how to love.

but now none of it matters because i can't forgive myself for any of it, i can't ever forgive myself for myself, and no amount of penance will ever take any of it back and my mouth feels hot with rotting food, and i just want to scream i just want to forget i want it all to stop or maybe i just need someone to hold me and say everything is ok, everything is ok but the very thought brings back images of the loves i've pushed away and the fear rises that maybe i'm doomed to be alone.

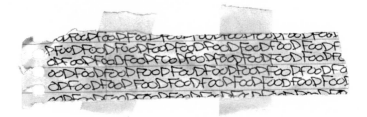

right away, i can tell something is wrong.

my eyes open, i'm staring into the sun, and i feel like i'm seeing things for the very first time. it's a struggle to sit up, my joints are sore and angry, my muscles tight. i'm having a hard time thinking straight, my mind clouded, and all i know for sure is that i'm really fucking hungry.

i try to get my bearings but i can't, everything's spinning, revolving around my hunger. i'm not sure how i got here or where i came from. i'm outside, the sun directly overhead, and i find myself wishing for the moon, longing for the cool darkness. i make it to my feet, i'm trudging along, grass underfoot, and i realize i'm not alone. there are others, and we're all marching towards a house a hundred feet or so away. i don't really look at them, but i can tell they're moving with the same grim determination i am.

the house is a two-story, someone's dream once, maybe, but now forgotten, not yet decrepit but well on the way. there is food in the house. i can feel it. there are many others near the house, some wandering aimlessly, some pounding on the walls, let me in, let me in. the yard's a minor battlefield, the grass trampled and forlorn, still corpses scattered here and there. a shot rings out and another joins them on the ground. someone has boarded up all the windows from the inside, doesn't want us to get in, is hoarding their food. we cannot have that. we must eat. we must survive. the hunger is overwhelming.

there's a man attacking the boarded window to the immediate left of the front door. he's a big man, work boots, black hair matted to his head. something's off about him, maybe his looks, maybe his movements, but i don't focus on him long enough to figure out what it is. i'm about ten feet away when i see a gun muzzle push through a gap between the planks, flash and bang, and the large man reels back, arm limp, shoulder destroyed. but he doesn't fall, he pushes back towards the window and the gun fires again, this time taking off a good chunk of the man's head as his flannel clad body falls into a useless pile without so much as a death twitch. the gun levels towards me, so i stumble left, almost falling over the lifeless body of a police officer. but it doesn't fire, and soon i'm past the window, lost in the others moving, circling around the house, all of us seeking, searching, needing a way in.

there's a woman, head cocked slightly to the side, she looks as if she's trying to climb the house, her arms above her head, her fingernails digging into the wall. her body moves with a mixture of anger and futility, her thick bedraggled blond hair whipping this way and that. her tight sundress shows off a body worthy of lust, if only i wasn't so hungry. i turn the corner of the house, she's out of view, and i'm confronted by the wreck of a car. the hood crumpled into the side of the house, the front windshield smashed, and what remains appears covered in blood on both sides. the car doors hang open like a mother who died during childbirth. a young man is trapped, his left leg crushed beneath the rear tire. he's clawing at his leg, an animal caught in a bear trap, his lips pulled back in an angry snarl.

another gunshot. beyond the car, two men and a child are standing on a slanted wooden cover to a cellar stairwell. it's chained shut, but the three of them are stomping on the wood, trying to break through. i start towards them. one of the men is wearing a mud covered suit, the kind worn by men pretending to be somebody. as i size him up, his foot crashes through the wood and he falls backwards, taken by surprise. his foot stays caught in the hole, and the sickly snap of bone tears through the air. it's a bad break, splintered white sticking through the tattered skin and fabric of his left leg. his face is one of confusion as he flounders on the ground, unable to free himself. the other two, an older man and the boy, are on him in an instant, forcing the crippled foot from the hole with merciless excitement in an effort to get in. the broken man seems shell-shocked, and tries to stand, quickly falling again to the sound of cracking bone and ripping flesh. he starts pulling himself along the ground with his hands, directionless, lost.

i move past him, forgetting him, focused on the hole he created. a way in. the man and the boy are attacking the wood around it, punishing it. another piece breaks loose, and the boy drops to his knees trying to rip it free with his hands. the man doesn't seem to notice, his foot comes down again and again, crushing down on the boy's hand. the boy raises it, staring at his ruined fingers, but by that point i'm at them, and i grab the boy from behind and toss him off the entryway. i'm hungry, beyond starving.

the man is relentless, he stomps down again, and a chunk of wood falls into the basement with a clatter. again, splinter and crack. again, and suddenly it all gives way, and the man disappears through into the darkness with a solid thud. i enter with a bit more care, slipping through to the concrete stairs beneath. i still manage to catch my left arm on a jagged outcropping, and it tears into me, but i barely notice. i'm inside, and that's all that matters. i find the man lying at the bottom of the steps. he looks broken, his neck, his leg, maybe his back. he doesn't look so much in pain as he does frustrated with his inability to move. he blinks up at me, but there's nothing i can or would do for him. his mouth and throat are caked in a dark brown dirt, he looks like a disgruntled monster, and i look away, focusing on the task at hand.

the basement is barely lit, sunlight pouring through the broken entryway and two very small and very filthy windows at ground level. i welcome this escape from the day, and appreciate the slight dampness in the air. the room is filled to the brim with forgotten antiques, once-loved toys, rarely used tools. boxes promising lost treasures are stacked everywhere. a narrow passageway snakes through the jungle of possession, leading to a wooden stairway that ascends into the house. i stumble through the basement, tripping but never falling over the junk.

my attempts at coordination give out when i reach the stairwell, and i collapse into the stairs and claw and crawl my way up them, banging my knees hard into the planks below, feeling splinters rip into my fingers as i reach above. at the top i find a flimsy door blocking my path. i pull myself to my feet, using the wall for support. i grab for the doorknob, but something's wrong, my hand misses and bangs into the door frame. i try again, fairing little better, i'm a mess of motor skills, as if i was drunk, except i haven't been drinking.

a rage grows in me. this door, this fucking door, stands between me and my salvation. it won't let me get to my food. i raise both arms, hands fisted, lean back, nearly losing my balance, and then tear forward with an anger all my own, my fists crashing against the door smashing it open, and i fall through, landing in a pile on the ground. a chair that must have been propped against the door lies to my side. no words can explain the sense of pure joy i feel at being so close to food, my insides crawling with unfettered hunger.

i'm laying on cold kitchen floor, a large oak table bearing down on me. soft light is filtering through the boarded windows, exposing a trail of torn and scratched linoleum leading to a massive old refrigerator, pushed up against the back door, blocking it. i hear someone pounding on the door, i can hear something rattling in the fridge, but there is no way anyone is getting in that way. it must have taken two or three people to push that fridge into position. a shot fires, it feels somehow closer now, and then another, and i hear a muffled shout coming from the front of the house but i can't make out the words, it's all garble, as if it's in some language i've never heard.

i crawl to a padded kitchen chair, using it to prop myself up, to regain footing. i immediately push off the chair towards the interior doorway. my momentum throws me against the far wall of a small passageway. it's covered in ratty wallpaper, once vibrant flowers now look dead and buried, i'm seeing everything in shades of gray. there are two open doorways to my left, and past them a carpeted stairwell on the right, leading up to the second floor. i hear, or maybe just sense, movement in the rooms to my left. then a shotgun blast, and i'm sure it came from one of those two rooms. i'm hungry, yes, but some sort of self preservation kicks in and i know instinctively to avoid these rooms. i can sense food upstairs, it's practically calling to me. i shamble past the first door, half seeing the armed men grouped together, peering out of the windows at the others massed outside. they don't hear me, my footsteps muffled by stained carpeting.

i can't blame them for protecting their food. but now i'm on the inside, i'm as good as them, better even, hungrier. and then i'm past the second door too, free and clear. the wide stairwell looms ahead, and i begin my ascent, using the handrail for support. i climb the stairs, on a mission, nothing can stop me.

when i reach the top, the house opens up into another long hallway littered with doors. most are open, but my undivided attention lies on the second door to the right. when i reach it, a wave of joy washes through my being at the sound of movement and muffled talking, or maybe weeping, inside. the door is cheap plasterboard. i throw myself into it once, hard, and i feel it fracture as i'm thrown back. again, and this time the door gives, and i'm through.

i take in my surroundings in an instant. a large quilted bed with an ornate frame is centered against the wall to the right. a mahogany dresser completes the sparsely furnished room. a man, warm, bleeding, lies asleep or comatose on the bed, his right arm hastily splinted and both legs bandaged with what looks like t-shirts. there's a woman behind the bed, staring at me in abject fear, her mouth open, screaming, maybe, but i don't hear her, and i'm not sure if it's because she's not making any sound or because i'm so close. behind her, huddled in the corner, are two children, little raggedy ann and andy, dirt crusted on their clothes and moist faces. i smile at them, or at least, i think i do.

the woman brandishes a large kitchen knife, bares her teeth, and rushes me. but now i'm in my element. i deflect her knife arm and grab her hair, pulling her head back hard and fast with a snap. and i'm at her throat, ripping, tearing, feeling the hot blood gush against my face, eating into her, making her mine. unfinished, but greedy for more, i drop her used carcass onto the floor, flaps of her skin still hanging from my mouth. i look over to see the children holding each other, crying, glowing with fresh warmth.

as i move towards them, i catch movement out of the corner of my left eye. i turn my head, and see the bedroom reflected in a large mirror built into the top of the dresser. there is a man standing there, staring back at me, and it takes a moment for me to realize that i'm looking at myself. i'm wearing blue jeans and a green t-shirt drenched in reddish brown. a huge chunk of skin and muscle hangs limp from my left arm. my stomach is torn open, and something that can only be intestines is pushing itself out. and my eyes, my eyes are sunken and gray against a pallid face, and death is staring back at me.

for the first time, i realize what i am.

a rain of gunshots downstairs, buried in an avalanche of screams. others must have followed me in. i hear a rustling behind me, and the corpse of the woman i slaughtered props herself up, one arm reaching up to grab onto a bedpost, her head hanging limply to one side. my hunger for her is gone, but i'm still nothing but starving. together, we take the children. they barely struggle, they don't even scream as we eat them.

and then suddenly, silence as everything recedes into meaningless echoes. all the blood and gore are gone, i'm alone, grinding my teeth, gulping down nothing. i go over to the bureau, but when i get there, i realize i'm standing in my bathroom. i study myself in the mirror above the sink, and i'm somehow different, warm, alive. my arm is miraculously healed. i run my fingers along my pockmarked face, feeling out of place. i meet my eyes in the mirror, and they burn into themselves with blue intensity.

i look down at my arm, where the flesh and muscle used to hang limp and useless. i run my other hand along the skin, massaging it, kneading it, gently at first, then harder, harsher, increasing the force until i'm hurting myself. i feel something under my skin. i dig at it with my fingers, and the lump is growing, pulsating. but it escapes my grasp, it recedes into me, and i feel it coursing through my veins.

there's a scalpel on the edge of the sink. i take it, and start an incision at my widow's peak, drawing the blade down my face, slowly, steadily, deep, thorough. down my forehead, between my eyes, continuing, splitting nose and lips, only stopping at the point where chin becomes neck. i look down, and the sink is painted red, but i'm not in pain. i let the blade clatter into the sink, reach up with both hands, and dig my fingernails into the incision and pull my face apart. the skin peels back easily as if it wasn't meant to be there in the first place, i'm discovering the alien within. i contemplate my new self in the mirror for a small eternity, until my eyes tear with violation, until i blind myself, the disobedient child staring into the sun.

92

click. i'm still alive, but i don't really feel any different.

my teeth are really starting to bother me. they ache. they whisper to me, you are getting old, you are falling apart, there is no way out of this, you will be as we are. and i'm screaming back at them, fuck you, i'll wrench you out you little bastards. i'll wear you as trophies around my neck, i'll curse your yellowed corpses with bloody spittle coating my words. and i know they're listening because the electric pain subsides and i can go on thinking.

i never thought things would turn out this way, i never thought i'd be who i am. maybe it's happening to someone else, maybe i'm watching tv. my hands look so human. i can see the thick veins riding the tendons like serpents as i move my fingers. i can see the scars but i can't remember exactly how i got them, only that i did. i feel my memory seeping away from me, i'm being forced to live in the now whether i want to or not. and i know everything is just a state of mind, but i can't find the reins, everything's spinning madly. i want to go back to the womb. i want to be part of someone else again.

i feel so impure, as if there's something inside of me that is defective or doesn't belong. something that forces me to be someone i don't want to be. i touch the lump on my forearm. i can almost see it pulsating. i get my toolbox and find a razor. i grab some bandages and antiseptic from the medicine cabinet while i'm at it.

i place the blade against my skin. it's cold and narrow. pushing it into my skin isn't easy. the skin depresses, it doesn't want to split. i push harder, and it feels like someone is pinching me. finally, the blade pierces through. now it's much easier, i'm drawing a line through me. i'm as careful as can be, but there is blood everywhere and it makes it so i can barely see what i'm doing. i've got an incision about an inch and a half long when i realize i have neither the knowledge nor equipment to stitch myself up afterwards.

he was right, it wasn't all that painful. but that changes when i force the wound open with my fingers, reaching into myself. my eyes are closed, i'm doing this blind, i'm trying not to think about it, i'm trying not to pass out. i can feel it. the lump. it's slippery, but i get a good grip and pull. i can feel it ripping out of me with every fiber of my being.

i puke all over myself. half digested food and stomach acids are all over my chest and arm, seeping into the wound. i'm retching at the sight of it all. and then the rest comes out of me, and i'm rushing to the bathroom leaving a trail of blood and vomit.

i don't even bother with the sink, i'm stripping naked in the shower. the water is scalding hot, i'm burning myself, but i need to get clean. the wound is screaming at me in waves of pain. the blood is still pouring from me.

i sit in the tub under the spray, and it hurts but i don't know what to do. i'm feeling lightheaded, almost giddy. and then i remember i'm bleeding. i get out of the shower and use a towel to dry my arm, sop up the watery blood. i retrieve the bandages and cover the wound, applying pressure until the flow draws to a trickle. then i take a new bandage and do my best to dress it properly.

i remember the lump. a sudden fear it was lost in all the commotion grips me with a harsh constriction of chest and stomach. but no, when i get to the table, it's sitting right there in a pool of blood and bile.

it's about the size of a quarter, but considerably thicker. i pick it up and examine it. i'm no doctor, but i think it's just fatty tissue.

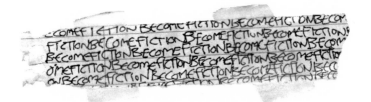

i'm feeling particularly disconnected and abstract and i need to ground myself, remind myself that i'm real. so i'm writing the thoughts i have down. not all of them, i leave out the day to day. but the rambling thoughts, i try to keep track of those to remind myself that i am thinking, that i'm going on. and on and on. but i can't think the way i want to.

maybe by writing the broken thoughts down, i can kill them off for good. on paper they become fiction, no longer real. i half expect to read through my notebooks someday and find some variant of *all work and no play makes jack a dull boy* over and over again. i think back to my notebooks full of sixes, and a shudder runs through me. if i can't even control my own thoughts then what's the point? am i me or am i just listening to a goddamn radio broadcast, this is my life? it feels like propaganda drowning everything else out.

you are the sunshine of my life, the subway man's singing. he looks pretty old, face sunk into wrinkles. he's fumbling at his guitar, his voice off key. he looks lonely.

i can't help wondering how many love songs have gone unrequited. sometimes, i feel that if i could put everything i am, everything i'm feeling into just the right words, if i could simply get across what i'm trying to say, truly express myself, the universe will click into place and everything will start to make sense. and i've tried. i've even thought that i've gotten it exactly right but i'm always left feeling garbled and misconstrued. and so when i hear something that makes me think, yes, they got it right, they found their words, i just want to know if it worked for them.

i'm falling away from people. i don't know how to communicate. no words carry the weight necessary to break through the wall of silence i've been creating for myself. the longer i go without speaking, the harder it is to find something worth saying. there are no words to use. if i could i'd create new words and use them instead. i'd fill in all the holes, all the gaps. i'd be able to get my point across. but i fear i'd just be speaking in tongues, sputtering gibberish, alone in my tower of babel.

i feel the noise of the city on me like insects, stinking of greed and aggravation and despair. i know this can't be right, i know there has to be more out there, words of love and devotion whispered from lover to lover, more songs such as the subway man was singing, but i'm becoming deaf to these things. everything else drowns it all out.

and i miss her so fucking much. i'm so sorry. i'm so fucking sorry and it doesn't mean jack shit. i'm tearing myself apart piece by piece and i want to stop, i want to think about anything but this, but i can't. i'm sorry. do you hear me? i'm sorry.

i suddenly realize i'm standing outside her building. i have no idea how i got here, i don't remember walking, let alone transferring trains. maybe it's fate, i need to talk to someone. i'll force the words out of me, water from a stone. but it doesn't matter, i'm ringing every buzzer in the building and no one is responding. she has to show up eventually, one way or another.

but i'm already walking away, and it's probably for the best. i wouldn't be able to confide in her. she wouldn't believe me. i wouldn't have anything to say. another day is over and i've got nothing to show for it. my thoughts are repeating like everything else, useless.

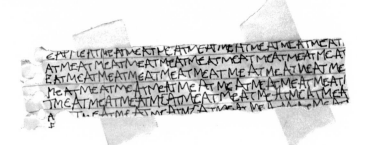

cockroaches are everywhere. they're in the shadows and they're climbing up my pants. i can feel them crawling across my face. i can feel them below the surface of my skin. i'm scratching at myself, jumping around, trying to figure out how to rid myself of them. a shadow of a man enters the room, unrecognizable, and he's telling me to stop fidgeting. but... but... but... i stammer and then forget what i was going to say. i realize no one's there and that i'm talking to myself.

i can't remember what i was doing, but i feel like this is a good thing. there's this buzzing in my head, almost painful. i want it to go away, but looking around, i can't find the source. if only the sound would go away, i'd be able to think straight enough to figure out what's causing it and then i'd be able to put a stop to it. it's shrieking at me, filling my head with barely discernible sixes. i notice a trap door in the room, so i pull on the handle and open it. i descend into darkness.

it's only now i realize it was the sound of people. they're everywhere, all around me, and i'm feeling paranoid because everyone's staring at me, discovering new reasons to hate me. i want to butcher them into silence. no, i'd never do that. i just want to make them all go away.

i realize i'm at the hideout again, and i know these people. and they're handing me a gun, and pointing at the door. i know what they want me to do. no no no no i'm thinking, it's not my turn it's yours. and they're all saying in unison, no, you don't understand, it's everyones' turn and they all show me their own identical guns.

before i respond the shadowed man comes back into the room. all the voices are silenced, and i look around to discover everyone in the room has taken on his appearance. i realize who they all are, they're the one who has been following me. they come at me, and they're shoving their guns down my throat, breaking my teeth, cutting open my mouth with their eagerness.

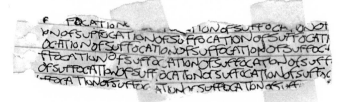

the day starts out in a cold sweat, my breathing a sort of suffocation. i'm frenzied with need to get the hell out of my apartment. i promise myself that today i'm going to be happy or die trying.

i am officially at war with myself, my own private oceana. i will kill every broken thought. i will choke them off at birth like miscarriage wrapped in umbilical cord, i will think something new and beautiful instead.

i throw on jeans and a shirt. i grab my notebook and a pencil. i don't shave or even brush my teeth, i'm slamming my door behind me. i'm riding the subways. underground is sort of safe zone—i'm not alone but i'm not outside, either. but eventually i can't take it anymore, i need air. nowhere is working for me.

trying to fight off the unwanted thoughts only seems to bring them into greater focus. my skin is cold, i'm shivering. i'm looking around at all these strangers and i feel the chasm between us all. i feel outside of them. there's nothing to say. their eyes are on me like plagues. i'm fighting the urge to race home, curl up in a corner, hide from it all, hide from their interpretations. i'm having a hard time not going fetal and collapsing right here.

every time i look away from something it starts melting. but i can never catch it, i whip my head around and everything is as it was. i'm pretty sure i'm talking to myself, but i can never quite catch myself doing it.

i'm wandering this world with my skull cracked open and my brain exposed, the curious few jabbing their fingers into the meat. i hear people shouting on the streets, invading my thoughts. i can't think because everyone else is too busy talking and i can't tell my thoughts from their voices.

i shrink back from the walls, feeling claustrophobic. the people, the crowds, are knocking into me. i need to find open spaces even if it means walking down the center of the road into oncoming traffic. i need to get away.

there's barely any warning, all of i sudden i feel it inside of me, right below my eyes, in the back of my throat and the front of my chest, in the pit of my stomach. i start screaming, angry, howling roars. the first one comes as a surprise to even me, but once i start i can't stop. i fall to my knees, doubling up. my screams rip through morning traffic, slowly overtaken by deep, wracking sobs. everyone is staring, no one knows what to do. i'm looking at some guy whose eyes are coated with appalled disinterest. people part around me like i'm an art fixture, they stare at me like i'm roadkill. nobody helps me up; a few minutes pass before i'm able to stand.

i need breathing room to recover so i escape the street into the shadows, sulking into the dark recess of an alleyway. i watch the people pass by without them seeing me, finding isolation in the midst of everything.

but even this isn't good enough, so i scale a fire escape to a tarred rooftop. the city breathes deep, a beast fat on recent kill. i'm watching the world go by and it's as if everything's already been decided and i'm just going through the motions, taking my damn sweet time to get there.

once again, i'm back where i started, always another broken promise. why must every path lead to the same destination? i walk to the nearest subway. take the sum of everything i am, of everything i've ever done, and all there is is a guy, alone in a deserted subway station in the middle of the night, fighting off the urge to break down in tears. how did i get here?

i want to be uplifting. i want to be able to tell people, live your life this way and you'll be happy. something will set you free. but as long as i keep coming back to this i know i'm full of shit.

maybe it's this city that's doing this to me. maybe i should go someplace else.

when i finally go home, i take out the gun. load it. deep breath, mind clear, i don't even count sixes, just pull real fast.

click.

click.

click.

click.

click.

i'm shaking, excited, and i pause only the briefest of pauses before i pull the trigger for the last time. the gun jams. i can't win for losing.

sometimes, all i can do is laugh. so i do, i laugh and laugh and laugh, i laugh until i can't remember why i'm laughing.

the streets are empty of cars but full of people. i'm looking up at the sky, it's full of billowy clouds, and i'm thinking, what a perfect day it is. and then i notice that the clouds are moving, faster, faster, and they all seem to be converging upon the same point in the sky far off in the distance. this massive ball of clouds is forming there, each of them adding itself to the mass, layering itself over the rest like a kid's used gum collection.

right about now, everyone else starts to notice this, people are stopping in the streets, turning, watching. and the sphere starts stretching towards the ground, and we're all entranced, and i realize it's starting to form a mushroom cloud. and i guess others must have come to the same conclusion i did, because the air fills with screams, and everyone's running, but for some reason no one is crashing into me, they all keep their distance, i'm the ripple in the crowd. i can't do anything but smile, because everything else seems so damn futile.

and i watch as rumbling gray death races towards me, and i'm thinking, so this is how it ends, and i'm wondering how many other nukes are right this second destroying the world. and i'm thinking, it figures, we deserve this. or, at the very least, i do. i lie down, in the center of the street, arms behind my head, relaxed, accepting, and i watch as the wave of extermination passes over me, only finally forced to close my eyes to avoid the stinging dust. and seconds, or minutes, or days later its finally ended, and i'm still lying there, alive.

i stand up, look around and find the city still standing, but now i'm alone with the streets. skyscrapers dot the horizon like gravestones.

there's a coffee shop to my left so i go inside. the art on the walls are covered with a dark charcoal soot, but when i go up to one and try to clean it off, i find it's really paint, it's meant to be that way. i go behind the counter to fix myself a cup of coffee, and then settle down on a stool. i'm looking out the front window at all the nothing going by, sipping. after i finish the coffee, i start to feel drowsy and put my head down on the counter.

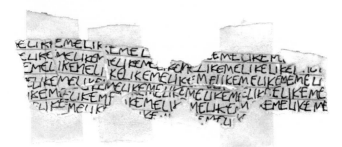

i decide to go grab some coffee. i'm outside the coffee shop, but i'm not going in. i'm forgetting something again, so i'm standing here, looking lost. people are passing me by, and i'm looking at each of them in turn, looking into their eyes.

everybody seems panicked. it spreads like a virus from eyes and mouth, the fear is building and it's thick in the air like humidity. the city is in turmoil, everyone's got something to say but no one knows how to say it, press time nightmares morphing into one another. it never ends, it never stops, but there is always one common factor—it's got fuck all to do with me.

i don't know where i'm going with this. i think i'm losing focus. i think i need to remember who i am right about now. i think i'm supposed to have a plot, but i don't even know what i'm supposed to be. all ambition and no direction.

i feel it in my stomach again, the sickness. i don't want yesterday to repeat itself. for that matter, i don't want anything to repeat itself.

there's a guy walking toward me, he's wearing a stylish suit. the kind of guy that probably wakes up looking that good. and when our eyes meet, everything changes. time liquefies, melts into itself. i'm in a loop, but this time i'm not alone. we're both here, aware, locked together. the revolutions don't end, i'm falling into his acidic blue eyes, faster, faster, faster than the speed of gravity, faster than sound, than light. and when the universe clicks back into place, when time jerks back into its normal flow, it's like being shot out of my mother and i fall like a brick to the ground.

before i can get my bearings, he's over me. i bring
my good arm up, reflexively protecting myself. when
nothing happens, i look up at him. he's standing there,
nonchalantly holding his hand out in support, and he's
saying you're new to this, aren'tcha. listen, he says,
i'm on my way somewhere but we need to talk before
you do some serious damage. you're a fucking menace,
you've got no control. and he pulls out this leather-bound
appointment book, pages through it and tells me to meet
him at the coffee shop we're in front of at noon tomorrow.
and then he's gone.

there are others out there like me.

there are others out there like me.

there are others out there like me.

i don't bother with coffee, i just start walking.

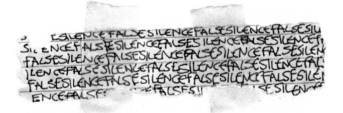

i'm at the assigned place at the assigned time, but he's
already there, sitting in the otherwise empty back room
of the coffee shop. he's exactly as i remember him. simple,
yet extreme in his elegance. he's stretched out, one leg
propped up on a chair, he looks as if he was meant to be
there, radiating. two coffees sit on the table in front of

him, steaming, the one away from him black just as i like it. i sit down, but i don't seem to register with him, or, at least, he doesn't bother to acknowledge me. i'm waiting, letting him make the first move, i've got a thousand questions but nothing to say.

i lean back in my chair and let my eyes wander. the art on the walls doesn't amount to much more than pretty crap, but at least it's obscuring the orange walls. one piece stands out, a large canvas, a man's face staring calmly out into the room. he looks rugged with just a touch of androgyny easing his features. the painting is nearly photo realistic, and it takes me a minute to realize his eyes are mountain ranges backed by blue skies.

there's a light fixture that sheds shadows of wings, a butterfly in reverse, jewel encrusted body with dull gray wings. some sort of large pipe snakes it's way across the ceiling, a docile python watching over us. a hole in the wall with the shape of a broken heart, small bitter cracks trailing away from it.

he reaches for his coffee, finally cutting through the false silence, when did it start? i've lost track, i'm not really sure, i respond. i'm not particularly good with time. you're dangerous, he's saying, you lack focus. yeah, you said that before, i snap back. i have no fucking clue what's going on. i'm not sure why i'm barking at him, i just feel this growing anger at the possibility that he knows something i don't. i relax my voice, maybe if you explain what's happening to me i can work on it.

he ignores my outburst, and as if to prove some unspoken point, he takes his time retrieving a coin from his pocket.

see that mug over there, he asks, indicating a mug a good fifteen feet across the room. just as my eyes focus on it, he flips the coin and i watch the perfect arc and soft revolution of the coin as it lands in the mug with a distinct porcelain clink. whoa. nice shot, i say, that was something else. he smirks, well, i missed a few thousand times. but i didn't let those misses happen.

he takes a slow drink of his coffee and lets the words flow out of him—no one i've talked to is exactly sure how it works or what exactly is happening, we've just compared notes and worked out a theory that feels right.

his voice is easy and flowing, almost hypnotic. but it's also relentless, never breaking or pausing, demanding no interruption. he's saying,

first off, some background. for most people, each moment in their life is defined by what they observe. they flip a coin, and they watch it go up, they watch it come down, and it's either heads or tails. what happens is what is.

but in actuality a moment is the sum of all the ways it could have possibly happened, just as a coin is both heads and tails regardless of which side faces up. every moment is shadowed by the infinity it was not.

this is where our gift comes in. for some reason, we can see the variations before one takes precedence over the rest and becomes the now. we are seeing the moment as it unfolds, rather than as it happens.

but more importantly, we have the power to guide the moment, to influence which possibility becomes actualized. doing this is sort of like juggling a chainsaw—you need to be able to focus, eliminate all distraction, so that when you see the iteration you want you can just reach out and grab it. every new moment is a victory in decision. think of the expert marksman: it's not that he hits the bullseye, it's that he doesn't miss.

every moment, no matter how seemingly inconsequential, exists in its totality. in order to fully reach your potential, you will need to be able to enter episodes at will.

he finally stops to take a breath. he eyes his coffee expectantly but doesn't make a move for it. i'm not sure i comprehended a damn thing he said, but i've etched his words into my mind, and i'm already poring over them again. but now i have a question and i want to ask it before he starts up again.

so what exactly happened when we met, i ask. we're generally able to see each other, he responds, it's in the eyes. but we're really rare so it's only an occasional collision—seeing me triggered an episode and i had to pull us out of it. when two of us are in it together, it's harder because of the conflict of wills. you'll see what i mean.

if you ever get your shit together you'll be a force to be reckoned with. see, this is what we're talking about here—if you can take control of your gift, the world's pretty much at your fingertips. you will become your own fate. his eyes sort of squint at me, a grin on his lips so subtle i might be imagining it. i just smile politely back at him, waiting.

or, he continues, you'll keep questioning yourself and start to wonder if i ever existed. if i was just some figment of your delusional mind. and maybe i am. maybe you'll crack and end up in an asylum somewhere, drooling and scratching at the walls.

yeah, i'm thinking, that sounds more my style.

there's one more thing i need to tell you, and it's important. you must learn to keep a low profile... you're lucky i'm the one who found you. there are others. more than a few have banded together and have used their power to rise to positions of importance. they do not see the need to share with anyone else. they don't want competition and will view you as a threat. to put it simply, if you are discovered you will be hunted down and slaughtered.

and with that, he's up and gone. i wonder if i'll ever see him again.

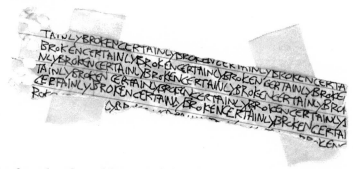

i take what he told me and decide to believe in it. knowing i'm not alone, that others experience the things i do, changes everything. it grounds me, allows me a trust in myself i didn't have before, recasting what was quickly becoming insanity.

i keep thinking back to the ones that went wrong, like the knifing, the biker. it's odd, the pent up guilt from those incidents has changed in tone. it's no longer fear but certainty that the outcomes were my fault. i didn't just let those deaths happen, i made them happen through my own lack of control. he was right, i'm a menace. i've been an unwilling participant in my own accidental murder spree. now that i know the loops can be controlled i will control them. i will practice. i will make them mine.

and i won't let myself be around others until i've figured this out.

i'm in my apartment staring at a wall of sixes and the small mug i've placed on the floor in front of it. i'm sitting on my ass about ten feet away, legs crossed, and i've got a quarter in my hand and a pile of change by my side. i've been flipping the coins incessantly, a small fortune scattered around the cup. a few have actually gone in, almost by chance, but i can't set off a loop and i'm getting frustrated.

i need inspiration. i go into my bedroom and get the gun out, loading it with a bullet. i spin the chamber and close my eyes, i concentrate past it all and soon i'm deep into the sixes. a deep breath and a pull of the trigger only to discover i'm still alive. the buzz of survival is a pale imitation of what it once was, but maybe it's enough.

fuck flipping quarters. i'm going to force myself into a loop. i look around my apartment for something threatening, anything, but nothing catches my eye. i leave my apartment. i'm in my boxers, practically naked, but it doesn't really matter. the stairs right outside my door lead down three flights, hugging the outer wall of the stairwell. the whole setup is surprisingly ornate—overly wide stained oak steps with a matching, deeply engraved banister. i look straight down the well and can dimly see the reddish tile floor of the foyer, grimy and used. there's definitely enough room.

i grab the railing with both hands, and pull myself up onto it, balancing. i'm a gargoyle crouching in the darkness. this is it, i'm thinking, and i spread my arms, my head full of vertigo, and then i'm falling.

miscalculation. i glance off of the second floor railing and hit the ground all twisted up. my leg rips in two, i can see bone sticking out about halfway up my left calf, screaming pain at me. i can feel warmth splattered across my face. it really fucking hurts. and then i'm falling again. i manage to break both legs this time. still falling, i break my nose on the floor. then i hit the ground and dislocate my shoulder and sprain my wrist. the next time, i shatter my right arm.

it takes hundreds of falls before i hit the ground in a safe roll. but then i'm falling again, it didn't click into place. and i hear the crack of my back breaking as i land nearly upside down. and i'm falling. it takes thousands more, a few relatively painless, before everything clicks into place. and i'm sitting and i'm laughing. my nose is bleeding from where i smacked it against the ground when i landed, but otherwise, i'm ok. not perfect, but good enough.

and then i'm up the stairs three at a time, up and over the railing, and i'm falling again. i don't stop until i've made the leap dozens of times. not all of them were painless. my nose is almost certainly broken. my left wrist is terribly sprained and i dislocated two fingers on my right hand.

my right knee feels like i cracked it in half. but those injuries are mostly from early on... i'm definitely getting the hang of it.

i open my eyes and i'm on a rocky beach, the waves crashing at my feet. the liquid horizon cuts across the night sky like infinity. i shed my clothes, throwing them to safety away from the tide. the water is warm as i walk into the surf, i'm up to my waist, and the sensation of the water swirling up against my skin makes the part of me underwater feel more complete than that exposed to the air. i'm a few hundred feet from the shore when i feel the ocean floor drop out from under me. i keep swimming, further and further, i want the land to be my new horizon.

my muscles are starting to tighten, and i start to wonder if i'm going to cramp up. i don't want to die out here, alone. i don't want to drown, i don't want to be found as ruined and bloated carrion washed upon the shore. but i keep swimming, each gentle swell lifting me and then letting me go. when i'm about a mile out, my foot kicks into something. a single word crystallizes my mind, leviathan. and then my other foot comes down on it, and i realize i've found a sandbar, a small island lost under the water. i can walk again, the water only up to my knees. i take a few steps and then sit down, legs crossed, my arms back, bracing me. the gentle swells don't threaten me, and i sit there for hours, contemplating, watching as the clouds roll in, obscuring the night sky.

it begins to rain, and i turn my face to the sky, eyes closed, and drink of it. when i reopen my eyes, i'm back on the beach near my clothes. i use them as a pillow, falling asleep on the rocks. when i wake, i'm lying outstretched on my bed. i feel sticky with salt and rainwater.

i haven't left my apartment except to run to the corner store for supplies. my phone is off the hook. my doorbell rang once, but i didn't answer it. i'd rather not be home. the lights were out so whoever it was left without further incident.

my injuries are pretty much healed, although i still have a slight limp and the faint aftermath of a black eye. the incision on my arm has left a scar, but i'm ok with that. at least it didn't get infected.

i've been practicing, honing my skill, an adolescent exploring his newfound sexuality. i'm an ace with the quarters. i make it every time, even with my eyes closed.

stopping a loop feels like stopping a fan with my hand. i just get in the way of the iterations, letting them work themselves into me until i find the one i want and then just... grab onto it with both hands and make it now. it's not as easy as it sounds, but it's not as hard as it sounds, either.

as i've learned to control the loops, i've become more able to think through them. that is, i feel layered over myself, as if i'm two people at the same time. i can hear the thoughts i originally had when i experienced the first iteration, all broken record like, but i also have another thought process that spans through them all. it's harder to hear, and sometimes it's a bit choppy and cluttered, a half-tuned radio station, a fractured narrative, but it's becoming clearer.

now that i have gained control, i don't feel as lost. i can think better. i feel powerful. i'm ready to reenter the world, but i can't say i'm not nervous. i've been inside for so long that i can't really remember how to deal with people. the thought of other people doing things, living their lives, sort of frightens me. but tomorrow, i'm forcing myself to go outside.

it would be easy to just let this be. i could revel in this. succumb to the greed. but i'm not going to use my ability to take what i want from the world.

at the same time i can't sit back and do nothing. i'm going to fix things. i'm going to make things right.

115

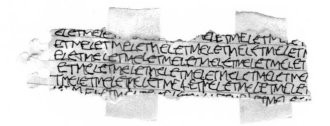

the sun is overhead, holding the earth in its loving grasp. i forgot how bright it could be. it hurts my eyes. i'm seeing everyone for the first time.

i'm not quite sure what i was expecting, but so far i'm not impressed. there aren't any loops. everything is just happening. i get some food. i wander some more. and then,

i watch as an old man doesn't fall to his knees.

later, i watch two large women screaming at each other, their words caustic and harsh. as i pass, one of them, ferocity consuming her eyes, is yelling rhythmically,

let me tell you
i will leave my blood here
it matters not

then her accidental poetry rescinds into careless vulgarity. i stand at a fair distance until their anger diffuses into apathy. and then i'm walking, they're gone. the gun was never pulled.

i smile. i keep walking. a man doesn't get hit by a car. a boy doesn't fall off his bike.

i'm a goddamn superhero. i am the averter, i am what did not happen. i see every possibility in front of me, i pick and choose the now. i make sure everyone's safe, i make sure no one gets hurt. and it's good. for once i feel like i'm accomplishing something. i'm making things right.

i'm at the top of my form and i'm already wondering what's going to go wrong. this is too good, something is going to fuck it all up. i wonder if i'll recognize it when it happens.

i watch everything go wrong. people die by the thousands, littering their corpses in my path almost as fast as i can blink them away. window washers splatter themselves ten feet in front of me, fat men choke their last breath on scraps of meat, elderly women mutter dying prayers as they cross their failing hearts, mothers not to be fall bleeding to the ground in miscarriage, children are destroyed by unswerving buses. few escape the wrath of my visions, i walk to the soundtrack of accident, to screams and deadly noise. behind me there is only the silence of the everyday. behind me, people just keep living out their lives. behind me, nothing happened.

i can remember a life in which these incidents were rare.

the first time i saw a dead body i was five. my memory as washed out as an old television show, the colors muted and slightly off—it was late at night, we were returning home. my father had made me roll down my window to help keep him awake against the gently hypnotic repetition of the road. the highway air was cold and harsh. his large hands were clamped hard around the steering wheel, his eyes wide as if he was trying to fit the whole world inside of them. his teeth clenched in this silent stare of must. stay. awake.

there was a solitary car in front of us. i remember watching it, wondering who was inside, wondering where it was going. i silently hoped my father would race it, race by it in a blur. we could be champions!

without warning the car in front veered hard left, glancing off the concrete center divider before driving full speed into the opposing wall in a terrific halt. it seemed as if it bounced back and forth across the road three or five or ten times, but i don't think it did. my father slammed on his brakes, his right arm reflexively swinging out and crashing into my chest to protect me. he knocked the air out of me, but it didn't really matter. we passed the wreck at a crawl. i could see the man inside. i remember thinking something was wrong with him, he was broken.

we didn't stop. my father's voice haunts me, there is nothing we can do, there was nothing we could do. he said this under his breath, i'm not sure it was meant for me even though i was the only other person in the car. i heard him as if he was shouting it.

it would be years before i saw another dead body, this time at a funeral. the old man looked plastic and fake. i broke down in tears, but not out of loss and grief—i was petrified at the thought that one day i too would be on display.

but now everyone is on display and i'm still the invisible one. bodies falling from the sky, my false vision forever armageddon. my mind is buried in their deaths. i know it's just phantasm, but i have the guilt of god on me, i'm wrapped up in responsibility like flypaper. i know most of what i'm seeing was never more than possibility, but i also know that if i stop paying attention, some small portion of it will actually happen.

i wonder which of the days' tragedies would have actually come to pass if i was without my gift. there is no way to know, but i'll let myself believe in the ones that come back to me in my dreams. i will take their nightmare visits as thank yous in absentia.

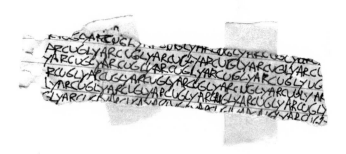

much later, i'm lying in bed, and i look around to see a group of elderly people milling about. they're my friends, but they all have the vacant stare of senility. i pull myself up to a sitting position, my back against the wall, shying away from them. how did this happen? where did all the years go? and then a strange, musty old man walks up to me and starts talking in words i don't remember. he's going on and on, and i look down and his ancient dick is hanging from his pants, a useless reminder of a younger day.

and as he's talking, he's pissing. it's mostly hitting the floor, but some of the spray is hitting my bed, soaking into my sheets, spreading, seeping. his piss smells like expired milk, and i start yelling, what the fuck are you doing, urinate on your own fucking bed you goddamn heathen. and he looks shocked, forlorn, as his eyes lower to his confused cock. he grabs for it, but the sudden motion redirects the stream and his piss rears up in an ugly arc and covers my face, fills my mouth. it's caustic and acidic, i can feel my teeth eroding, crumbling away. and i start gagging, spitting out the foulness, but my saliva turns into more of his urine, and i'm spitting and puking up his piss, and the old have congregated around me, and they're all pointing, laughing.

the day hits me like a sucker punch, i come screaming to the surface with nightmare already forgotten. the room has nothing but emptiness to offer, i'm shaking, my fists clenching sheets. where am i? and then i remember. i need to get outside. i need to fix things before they go wrong.

i'm realizing this is all much more intense than i thought it would be. how many ways can you watch someone die, only to have them walk away, smiling? no thank yous, no acknowledgment. when people on the street look at me right after i fix something, echoes of the click still reverberating deep through me, i know they see my wide, seeing eyes and they're thinking, creep. crazy. nutjob. and as they think it, so do i, our voices silent in unison.

how do people know if they've lost it? insanity is internally consistent. whenever i go outside i'm wearing my sanity like a cheap halloween mask. reality has cracked and it's spewing its insides all over me, everything is unraveling right in front of my eyes and i don't know how to keep any of it together. i'm lost in the moment, a stuttering strobe light illuminating the future before me.

i can't make sense of what i'm experiencing and i'm not sure if the glitch is in the universe or in my head. the loops hit me like flash floods, consuming me.

i see so much that i'm losing track of what's actually happening, lost in possibilities. my memory, gorged on countless nows, is ceasing to be able to distinguish between any of them. i can't remember which iteration really happened, i'm not even sure if any of them did. life has become a montage of the unreal. maybe the universe is lying to me. and i let it all out, i read into things that aren't there, i vomit up my own choice delusions. i must appear to have a severe case of tourette's, jerking and fidgeting, reacting to everything that didn't happen.

i can feel myself going in and out of focus, at times cogent, at times scattered and tangential. i don't know what to do about this or how to fix it. my thoughts are focused and sharp yet fleeting, easily forgotten. i am not secure enough in my sanity for any of this. i recognize my own psychosis yet i'm helpless against it. what if i'm imagining all of this? and what if the looping is the only part of me that's sane? what if it's my lack of acceptance of this simple truth that's causing all the trouble?

it feels almost cliché to wonder about my own sanity, but i don't totally trust myself. i can't help visualizing my uncle ripping his son apart. is the game rigged? i want so much to be able to control myself, to claim ownership of my mind, but maybe it's genetic, inescapable. when do i stand up and ask for help? it goes against every fiber of my being. who would i even ask? i won't let myself give up, but in the process i'm tearing myself down.

if i could walk down the street with my eyes closed i would. i'd gouge out my eyes and face the world with scarred, gaping holes.

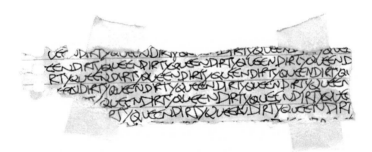

the dirty queen is singing, save the last dance, muthafuckkkkaaaaa. you can't buy shit like me for all the dollars you've got, muthafuckkkkaaaaa. she's looking straight at me from across the subway tracks, saying, i could be somewhere else right now, and i wouldn't have to look at you, you goddamn sonuvabitchhhh.

she's the subway sensation, the center of attention and she knows it. i don't share my liquor with no one, muthafuckkkkaaaa. my mother was a nurse, and she'd kick all yer asses just for breathing wrong.

she stands, her timeworn body covered in soiled clothes little more than rags. her eyes are too small. she points in a stagger, her finger swaying across the platform in universal accusation, i'm talking to you, muthafuckkkkaaaa. you and all your kind, you goddamn sonuvabitch.

these last words are devoured by the roar of train between us. it pulls up to a screeching halt, it's doors open and welcome me in. i watch her through the window as the train pulls away.

for all my power, there's nothing i can do to save her.

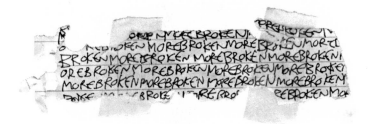

i should be happy that i'm making a difference but the more i fix things, the more broken i am. i fear i'm doing the wrong thing. i'm a factory, corruptive, corrosive, carelessly encroaching on the future no matter how softly i tread. i feel wrong wanting anything more than what is, that i'm polluting the now with my will. i don't want motives, intentions, agenda, i just want to be. but how? how can i deny the wanting? shouldn't i fix what i can?

it's bad enough that i can't be everywhere. i wish i could multiply myself. i can't fix what i can't see, and i want to fix everything. i have a taste of control, and now i want omniscience. i can see the madness in all of this, in me, but i can't do anything about it. even with the now at my fingertips, i can't escape futility.

i feel like the sun, feeding the all while burning myself out. except without an earth, all i have is void. potential by itself is worse than nothing. i'm the semen crusted on the sheets. i'm so lonely and it's the one thing i don't know how to fix.

the phone is ringing, and i know it's her. it's been ringing constantly all day. it woke me, and i've been sitting next to it, watching it, wondering how long she can keep it up. the handset is warm from my grip. my other hand is shaking with madness. i never know if a ring will be the last and i suffer with anticipation as each recesses into nothing, teasing me with silence, before the next rips into me again, digging further into my skull.

i wasn't going to call her, ever. i really don't think i would have. but i know it's only a matter of time before i pick it up. i can't break the cycle any more than she can.

there's a pause between calls, and in the brief respite i remember to breathe. and then it begins again, ringgggg. ringggggg. ringgggg, grinding into my head. i pick it up. hello? all i can hear is crying, and then a sniffle, her voice cracking, i miss you, i need to see you.

i want to slam the phone down. i want to tell her to fuck off. but i can't find that voice, so instead i'm making plans to meet her in an hour at the park. of course she comes back. of course i let her. i don't know how this happens. i don't know why i do this to myself. why we do this to each other. maybe sometimes we're so scared of things ending that we keep even those things best thrown away.

i take my time getting to the park. i keep stopping, looking in store windows, fumbling around in my pockets as if i'm looking for something. i want to be late, i want her to have given up on me.

by the time i finally get there i wish i was somewhere else. hi! she's running towards me, hugging me, practically jumping with joy. you'll never believe what just happened! a squirrel came up to me and rubbed against my leg! she's acting as if we never parted, as if we've never had anything but this. her enthusiasm is alienating me, it makes me feel somehow wrong for not feeling the same way. it was all small and fuzzy and i wish i had something to give it but i didn't! i try to say something in response but i can't muster up a thing.

so i sort of keep walking and she falls into step alongside me. she takes my hand in hers and squeezes, and when i look over at her she's smiling up at me. and despite my better judgment, i smile back at her, her elation spreading like contagion. i can't stay upset, i can't stay distant from her. damn it, i don't want to be happy. not this way.

we sit across from each other as if we've known each other forever. we smile as if we mean it. except i don't. i feel it stretching across my face and it worries me. it doesn't match the dread inside my chest and stomach, the tension between my eyes.

how do i get into these situations? i keep jumping off of cliffs and then realizing life is worth living. i've trapped myself in her again and i don't know what to do.

i can see my patterns and i don't know how to avoid them. it's almost as if i'm aiming for them. it wouldn't be so bad if they weren't so destructive.

i know she wrecks my head. i know it. i know it. yet i invite her back into my life as if somehow it's going to be different this time. and i only realize it's not after it's too late. one thing is for sure: i need to escape her. again.

she reaches across the table and takes my hand in hers. i don't know how to react, so i don't.

i love you, she says. i missed you.

i can't function, let alone speak. i can't hear my thoughts over the screaming in my head: get away, get away, get away.

that's ok, she's saying, you don't have to say anything. i know you love me too.

my entire being feels corrupted and foul. i don't like the way i'm thinking.

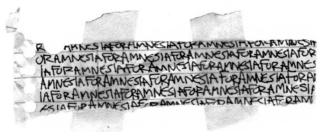

i long for amnesia. i want to start over. i've made so many mistakes in my life, i feel buried in them, dirt forcing itself into me, suffocating me, fingernails bleeding from the constant digging. i don't even know which way is up.

i want new thoughts, because mine are stinging me with their venom. they're weeds overrunning a neglected garden, strangling my ability to be happy and sane. if only i could kill these thoughts, i'm telling myself, i'd be ok. but no matter how hard i fight them off, they always return, compelling me to destroy everything beautiful in my life, burn it all to the ground. i have created a monster in myself. i love as i destroy, i destroy as i love.

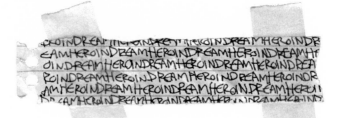

she's curled up fetal, almost childlike in form if not in appearance. ever the savage pixie, her arms covered in shadows like angry ink. her hair is all knotted up in something approximating dreads, the sides are shaved and chopped, a random mess of blond. wisps of hair inch down the nape of her neck. she's wearing combat boots, a black shirt, a beautiful blue ankle length skirt that has a gentle off-white floral pattern. it's frayed and patched in places with more holes needing fixing.

neither of us has said anything for hours, and while i'm wide awake, she seems almost catatonic. and then i'm straining to hear every last syllable, her gentle voice barely audible over the hum of the city. her voice is so low that i'm not even sure if she knows she's speaking aloud. it's a story, it's a poem, it's everything, all else is nothing. her words consume me, they are my entire reality. so beautiful. smooth. hypnotic. for a few minutes, i silence an entire city just to hear her, to live inside her words.

i wish that i could have written her words down as she said them because even now only one word stays with me:

phoenix.

a title for a poem with words long lost. i want to sit in silence, in respect of the moment. eventually, though, i simply have to know more. as quietly as i can, i ask her about it. she doesn't even recognize the magic of her words. that wasn't anything, she whispers, just a heroin dream.

i open my eyes and she's wrapped up with me. i could have sworn i kicked her out last night but i guess i didn't. her legs are parted around me, her warmth against my thigh. it's hard to resist pushing myself into her, but i don't want to wake her. enough damage has already been done.

i climb out of bed and walk barefoot to the bathroom, the floor pleasantly chilled. i look at myself in the mirror and see a monster. ragged hair, thick circles under my eyes. i shave quickly, nicking my chin a good one, then jump into the shower to rinse off and wake the rest of the way up. i keep the water like ice.

when i go back into the bedroom, she's awake. she's sitting on the bed, my gun in her naked lap. i found this in your drawer, silly! what is it?

a gun. i feel stupid answering, but she's the one who asked.

wow. is it loaded? i feel sort of strange telling her there's only one bullet, so i lie, no, it's not. i don't want to have to explain my habit. i just have it for show, in case i get robbed or something.

oh. i can barely watch her as she peers down the barrel. you shouldn't do that, i warn her, it's dangerous. why? you said it wasn't loaded, silly. i'm not sure how to respond to that without incriminating myself, so i say nothing.

do you know what you said to me last night? no... what? you woke me up, and you said, in this matter of fact voice, i should charge admission for my dreams. that's just how you said it, all serious. then you fell back asleep. you were sooo cute.

and she aims the gun at me.

sometimes when i see something falling i react without thinking and catch it. other times, i'm frozen in place, just sort of watching it fall, unable to will myself to move. this is one of those times.

she pulled the trigger, and in her little elven voice yelled, pow! (sixteen point six six six repeating) i just stood there, incredulous, as she shot me again, pow! (thirty three point three three three repeating) my mouth was open but i couldn't form words, pow! (five oh point oh oh oh repeating) then she giggled, aimed the gun at herself, and blew her fucking brains out. (sixty six point six six six repeating)

i see this in the past tense, because i knew it was going to happen before it actually did. i was looping the entire time, i watched it all fall into place. i should have altered it, but i couldn't find my control. instead i just let it happen, passively, mindlessly flipping channels through possibilities, none of them meant for me. maybe i even made it happen. i'm not sure. it's my fault, one way or another.

her body is twisted on my bed, spun from the force of violence, legs spread, her ass aimed up towards me. it's the most obscene image i've ever seen, my eyes drawn up her curved back, her shoulders and neck hanging off the splattered bed, chunks of her are sliding down the wall. i can just make out the remains of the side of her face. she doesn't look so beautiful anymore. i can't help but be reminded of the first time i saw her.

i'm not sure how long i stand there staring at her defiled body. i keep expecting police to crash down my door. i keep expecting something other than the sounds of blood.

this wasn't supposed to be how it ended. i can't breathe. i already miss her.

i'm not really sure what to do with her body so i just leave it there. i need to go for a walk. i need to think. this is wrong. this is wrong. this is wrong.

it's a mystery, and i can't figure out who did it. there's a
body, decapitated, lying in the next room. no one knows
the corpse, as unknown in death as he was in life.

i look around at the people in the room. at the woman,
her face given in to wrinkles and anger. she looks serious,
but the gaudy blue pendants dangling from her ears
contradict her. there's a man, crooked with cane, he's
wearing shorts with white socks pulled up past his knees.
he's got dark shadows underneath his blue eyes cloudy
with cataract, wisps of gray hanging flat from a liver-
spotted scalp. there's a girl, athletic, long brown hair tied
back with a bandanna. there's a guy in his twenties, he
looks intelligent. his slim glasses make him look like an
engineer. a boy, strawberry blond bangs overhanging his
eyes, picks silently at his nose.

i could go on about the rest of them littering the room, but
really, it doesn't matter. and i'm thinking, they all look
guilty. each and every one of them is hiding something.
each and every one fears being found out.

i take center stage and the words fall out of me as if i'm
reading from a script, ok, no one leaves this room, there's

a killer among us and we're going to figure this out. first order of business, we've got to find the head. so we're all searching but there isn't much to search. there are only the two rooms, this one and that one. both are fairly minimal in furnishings. the one we're all in is a library, endless rows of books staring out at us, but none that i recognize. we tear them all from their shelves, until there's nothing but a pile of jumbled words on the floor. we find nothing, no secret compartments or rooms, no clues.

on to the next room, the shag rug sticky and matted with pooled blood, the headless body, bare walls, and a television set. we're all standing around aimless, there's nothing to search, until someone thinks to turn on the tv. and there's the head, staring back at us. we congratulate each other on finding it, waiting expectantly for it to say something, for it to identify its murderer. but there is only snow and static, and after a few minutes of abject silence someone gets bored and starts changing the dial. but the head is on every channel and still has nothing to say. finally i've had enough, and i'm yelling turn it off, turn it the fuck off, enough already. someone complies, and then we're left with accusatory words tossed carelessly around the room, fingers pointing in every direction. they're all at each other's throats. there is pushing and shoving, violence erupting. and i'm watching these people interact, and i'm falling away, i don't understand them, i don't get it. i just want them to find peace with one another, or maybe just to shut the fuck up for a second so i can think. but there's no solution to the problem, no way to resolve a damn thing, so i do the only thing i can think of. i lie. i'm yelling above them, stop, stop, you're all wrong, i did it. i'm the guilty one. and as they tear me apart with dirty fingernails, i wonder if i'll become their martyr.

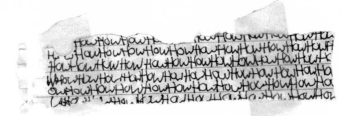

i've been roaming the streets. i can't concentrate. i have no idea how much time has passed, everything is now. i sleep so rarely i can't remember if i am. i stink, i can smell it and i see it in the faces of people that pass me by. i feel half dead, some inner part of me is barely there, or gone completely. i'm fighting for a life i don't actually possess.

as i walk, the crowd parts for me. i know it's not out of respect, but i'll accept it as such anyway. they know not what i do, how much i've seen. i feel ancient. i've lived far too long, my years stretched like canvas.

i see my mentor out of the corner of my eye as i'm walking by an electronics store. or at least, i'm pretty sure it's him, his face briefly frozen in the upper left corner of the six o'clock news. i can't hear any sound through the glass of the storefront but the bold text layered across the screen pretty much spells everything out: "federal manhunt ends in bloodshed." they found him. they found him and they killed him.

the video cuts to a man in front of a microphone. he looks exactly as someone doing a press conference such as this one should, with wide angular cheeks, a dark rippled brow, blood red lips. hair slicked back with comb marks locked in hardened gel. the text at the bottom of the screen identifies him as a federal agent. then i notice the guy standing just behind him. i recognize his eyes. i'm sure i've seen that fucker before.

or at least i think i have. but then the image is gone, replaced by the smiling vacuum of commercial.

the next morning, he's the headline. they say he was a murderer. they say he was a lot of things. at least one is true: he's dead.

i have one question: how the fuck did they kill him?

i'm pretty sure i'm being followed. there's this guy. he's following me, i'm sure of it. i keep catching him out of the corner of my eye but whenever i look nobody's there. i sometimes see him in the reflections of store fronts. i'm a mouse in a labyrinth. i'm being watched. studied.

i draw him, the sketch jumbled together from a collection of glimpses. i'm always erasing parts, replacing, trying to make it perfect. when the sketch gets too dirty and smudged to continue, i start over on a new piece of paper from where i left off.

i've almost got him locked down. i can almost see him. he looks pretty normal. brown hair, just a few inches long but wild, unstyled, like he had forgotten to brush it that morning. blue eyes. long nose, thin lips, overly narrow face. scruffy, unshaven. i erase his nose and try again. it's slightly more accurate this time. i think i've got his eyes exactly right, but i've thought that before. i might need to make them a bit larger.

i catch a glimpse of him while hidden in an alleyway, so i fix his eyes some. as i'm sketching, i'm nodding off every few minutes. so tired. my eyes feel like molten cores, burning and heavy. i haven't been back to my apartment—i can't let him know where i live. besides, she's there. waiting for me.

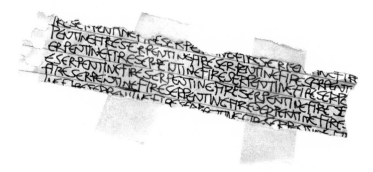

the alley walls are brick, covered in serpentine fire escapes and boarded windows. the alley itself is narrow, the ground littered with piss soaked newspaper, needles, and other refuse of the damned. i'm feeling claustrophobic, i need to get out. i went this way for a reason, but as the walls close in on me i can't remember what it was. i'm threading through the maze of passageways, feeling lost, even though at each intersection i always seem to know which way to go.

i hear voices behind me, and realize it's dark out and i shouldn't be here. this place is dangerous. i pick up my speed, faster, faster, until i'm running, until i'm breathless. i'm throwing myself into my escape, turning corners with abandon, left, right, left, left, right. and then i turn a corner and run full force into him, we're tangled together, and i'm all apologies. i look him in the eyes, and all i see is anger fused into his face. he's reaching for something, and i'm thinking, so this is it.

i hear the gunshots from miles away. my body is lifted, gut shot, and i know i'm already dead but i still feel myself falling. the guy doesn't seem to care, i'm cheap to him, worthless, and as i hit the ground my eyes open with a gasp.

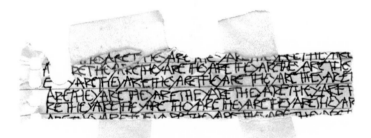

i wake up in the alleyway, gagging. i must have passed out from exhaustion. if i didn't reek before, i do now. the left leg of my pants is soaked through with an unknown foulness leaking from a dumpster. my sketch lies crumpled and wet by my side. i shove it into my pocket, saving it from its demise. i'll have to start a fresh one. a better one.

from the feel of the city it's probably morning rush hour. i can hear voices and footfalls coming from the street. i'm not really sure, but as i exit onto the sidewalk i think i see the guy who's following me standing across the street, half buried in crowd. a deep shiver runs through me, he's looking more and more like my drawing. i'm going to have to touch up the jawline, maybe. but a bus goes by, blocking the view, and then both are gone. i can't go home. but i need to go home, wash the stench off me before i heave up my guts.

i'm trying to decide what to do when i see a woman, she's rushing to cross the street but the light has already changed. there's a taxi, it's racing at her. i focus, i can see how close it's going to be, so i reach into the moment to fix it. i'm right, so many horrible things are unfolding and when i see the now i want i take hold of it, but something's wrong... i'm fighting for it, but i can't make it click into place and i watch as it's replaced by violence. every time i try to stop the loop it's as if the iteration is snatched out of my grip.

i'm swimming in potential tragedy. i concentrate harder, and with every ounce of energy i have i force the click. it's loud and sharp, i feel it hit my bones. and everything continues past the moment as the taxi swerves around her, just an inch from clipping her, honking wildly. that was much harder than it should have been. i almost lost it.

suspicious, i look around just in time to see him melting into the pedestrian traffic. so that's it. they're on to me. i was just tested. they must have suspected me. now they know for a fact. he was in the loop too, forcing me to struggle for it in a battle of wills. i wonder if i won because i was stronger, or because he let me. after all, she wasn't the target, just bait.

i think back to what my mentor told me... they are going to come after me. they're going to slaughter me. i need to get away.

the words reverberate in all their variations: they're after me. they know. they found me.

i'm racing back to my apartment, because today is the day i'm disappearing. i have no other choice. the crowds are parting for me, the running, reeking man. i'm banging into them anyway, bouncing off them, moving, moving. people are chasing me with curses.

i'm through intersections without looking, left, right, left, left, right. i hear cars more than see them, and they don't seem to be hitting me because i'm still running.

and then i get tackled. i come down hard, jaw cracking against pavement, teeth breaking into each other and ripping through my gums, but i'm already looping, coming down again and again in a tangle of limbs. and finally i'm able to dodge the tackle and my assailant flies past me and i let everything click into place. i'm on my feet before he is, and i see that he's in uniform, he's a cop.

he's after me, he's working for them. they're after me. he's making his way to his feet when he trips backwards into the street, falling flat on his back. he's lying there, looking up at me with a confused look in his eyes when a truck crushes into him and cracks his skull open like an eggshell. now the moment is already past, it's too late to do a damn thing about it. and as i'm running, people are screaming and i'm screaming with them.

i'm in my apartment. her stench is overwhelming, i try hard not to look. i'm showered and changed in record time.

backpack. check. boxers, socks, toothpaste, toothbrush. check. the cleanest t-shirt i own. check. a roll of toilet paper and a towel. don't panic. don't panic.

i go through my wallet, destroying all identification. i destroy my credit card, i can't leave any sort of trail. i'll empty my bank account at the nearest atm and then i'll destroy that card too. is that everything? yes, i think it is. i'm closing the door when i remember. i rush back in and grab the first book i see, and then i'm out.

i figure i've got a slight advantage, i look completely different now that i'm all cleaned up. i can even think a bit straighter.

i'm on the subway, i'm at the bus station. first bus anywhere, please. thank you. you have a nice day too, ma'am. and soon i'm out of the city. the seat isn't supposed to be comfortable, but for once i have no trouble falling asleep.

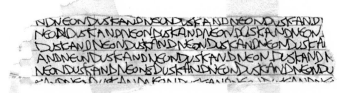

i'm crashed out on the bed, fully dressed and half asleep. the motel room is pleasant, sort of. there are horrid green curtains blocking out the sun, clashing with the grossly vibrant floral pattern on the wall. if i was going to keep a journal, i think i'd start by pasting in a scrap of wallpaper from each motel.

i'm moving anonymously, keeping off the grid. i can't stay in one place too long. i don't know how easy i am to track down, but i'm sure they're trying to.

i'm living on next to nothing. i've been thieving almost all my food. it's nice not having to worry about getting caught, but i feel sort of bad using my ability so selfishly. i don't know what else to do. my mentor (damn, why don't i even know his name?) was right, i could have the world at my fingertips. then again, i could also be dead like him.

i stick to canned goods and things i can eat cold, except when i'm staying at one of the rare motels where there's a hotplate or kitchenette down the hall. this one place, they had their heat on even though it wasn't cold outside and i'd just sit a can of whatever on the radiator. it tasted much better than it ought to have.

right now i'm sitting here eating tuna fish straight out of the can with a dirty plastic fork. i don't have a plate, and i didn't think to score bread or mayonnaise. it's not so bad, really. it was a bit dry, but few packets of ketchup solved that.

i need to get out of this room. i throw the empty tin into the small wastebasket near the bathroom door and gather my clothes from the floor, putting them on. and then i'm outside, walking away from the motel. it's a dysfunctional child's doll house in the dim dusk and neon light.

i want more than this. tonight's going to be my last night in this town, i've already been here too long.

as i move from town to town, i have the illusion of destination. if i'm going somewhere, i must have a purpose. there must be a reason. escapism as realism. i wonder if i'm living the rest of my life.

the only thing that really bothers me about these towns is that there isn't much to fix. it's not city and everything just works a little better here. not as much broken behind the scenes. not so many knots. i never thought i'd miss the city, but i do. during the quiet nights, i just want to hear a siren slicing through everything.

i spend the day sitting at a bus stop. it's not that i'm going somewhere, it's that i have no place to be. besides, it's interesting watching the people. sometimes i talk to them.

i decide to take a woman home. saying all the right things doesn't exactly come naturally but in the end that's all i do. i'm not sure if this technically qualifies as taking advantage of her. is it still her choice even if i ensure the outcome?

in the end it's a disaster. she's lying there, naked, and i want nothing to do with her. i feel ill at the thought of touching her, let alone being inside of her. all i see is her ruined smile, her cheek ripped open showing broken teeth at odd angles. and now she's yelling at me, angry at me for not wanting to fuck her.

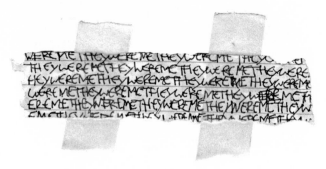

i'm pretty sure today is thanksgiving.

as much as i've always slagged holidays, right now i'm thinking it wouldn't be so bad to be gathered round a candlelight table, surrounded by family and loved ones.

i consider going to a diner. i could be that guy, sitting lonesome in the window, the renegade holiday martyr. who am i kidding, i am that guy. as a kid i'd always slow down my pace to watch them eat, sometimes even stopping, leaning up against the glass as inconspicuously as i could. i knew, even then, that they were me.

it takes me about an hour walking the strip mall highway before i find a diner. as soon as i enter it i know i've made a mistake; this is the saddest place i've ever been. copies of me are placed strategically around the establishment, the gaps filled in by families too poor to eat anywhere else. the silence of the loners stands in stark contrast to the bickering of parents and the holiday cheer of grubbing children.

the seat for me is obvious, corner, up against the front glass window. i lean back against the window, stretching one leg out along the cushioned bench thick with cigarette burns. there are huge stretches of sticky fabric tape coming loose, half-assed repairs against the onslaught of age.

the table still has someone else's dinner on it. fat red lipstick and blackish grease smears the coffee mug in front of me. the meal looks practically untouched. the plate on the opposite side is the exact opposite, bones picked clean like carrion.

the waitress would look at home on television, her mouth chewing on nothing. you can see the indent of where the cigarette should be. let me get this for you honey, she's saying, clearing the table. a quick wipe-down leaves arcing trails of gravy. i can smell her leaning over me, cheap perfume and a day's work. what're you doing alone tonight, hun, she's asking. i'm traveling. got a girl back home? i don't respond, trying to cut the conversation short, turning my head away from her. i can see her eyes in the reflection of the window as she shoves a menu in my general direction.

i feel bad. but it's simple, really. i'm here, alone. let me be. let me be alone. if that makes me an asshole, so be it.

i order like a true professional, a little bit of everything. it sounds so good on the zeroxed 'thanksgiving special' menu, turkey with stuffing, mashed potatoes, yams, cranberry sauce... unfortunately, the actual meal is little but disappointment. the yams are the closest to good, but even they're a bit dry. the cranberry sauce tastes acidic, i don't even bother with it past the first taste.

i spend the meal moving food around my plate, staring at the large head of a child across the room. he's staring back at me with gluttonous eyes, his face dripping gravy, chunks of turkey pasted to his chin.

all is forgiven with the coffee and pumpkin pie. the coffee is perfect diner coffee, hands down. the pie is so good i get another slice.

i'm sharing this motel room with cockroaches. they're everywhere that i'm not looking, i listen to them scurry through the night. the scent of dead mouse masked by rain forest air freshener. interior decoration by the blind, color scheme of the damned. i've been here way too long, but one more night shouldn't hurt. i've got the television on, and i'm flipping through the channels. i never stay on any station for more than five seconds, and about the twentieth time through the spectrum i flick it off. they've made me into a murderer, i saw it on the news.

the bed makes me feel like i'm dying. i'm sinking into the mattress, it's sucking my life away. this is by far the worst motel i've stayed at. but the proprietors seem to agree—it's also the cheapest. the first night i was here a woman knocked on my door, trying to sell herself. i declined, but it's still sad to think about.

i can hear people screwing through the wall, maybe the guy next door took her up on her offer. i reach for the remote, i'd rather listen to anything else. but then there's a shocking noise, almost obscene, a mix of crashing violence and splintering wood. the door, it's caving in on itself. raid. they've found me.

i fall into a loop. and somehow, i'm moving before the door even starts to break. i'm throwing myself through the window, falling two stories again and again but finally landing in a roll, up and running in one swift motion. and it clicks into place as the surprised officers start yelling at me, halt, police!

but i'm not halting, i'm running. halt or we'll shoot! and i hear the sound of gunfire after i already feel the punch of the first bullet in my shoulder. and i'm looping, i'm taking it back, i'm dodging left to the sound of a bullet whizzing by me, to the sound of the click. i can't take a step without needing to loop, i'm shot countless times and not at all. i'm half wondering what would happen if i got shot in the back of the head... would i die or would i still be able to get to another iteration of the loop? i find out quickly, too many bullets flying for it not to be a possibility.

and when it happens, i am the darkness. and then the light. and the head shot is just another bullet flying by my ear.

147

a few streets away, i hitch a ride. it was easy; the first words out of the man's mouth are, you're lucky kid, i don't normally pick up hitchers. he looks athletic, young for the obvious years his face betrays. something about him reminds me of my grandfather. not too tall, but built kind of like a bulldog. his short white hair is arched back neatly from a strong widow's peak, but it looks ready to fly in all directions at a moment's notice.

we're in his pickup and we're speeding away. where ya goin' kid, he asks. i don't really have an answer for him, so i just chuckle, away from here. he smiles, he's got this grand smile, a real one that hits me deep. he starts right into conversation, i got this three year old gran' daughter, he's saying, she's a beaut, she is! you wouldn't believe it.

used to be, i hitched everywhere, but nowadays you're lucky i picked you up. not sure why i did, musta been something about you that reminded me of me. used to be, you didn't even have to lock your doors at night. but nobody trusts no one anymore, an' people are happy to oblige by being dirty theivin' crooks. this world, my boy, is goin' to the shitter.

i ain't sure where we went wrong, but i know we screwed the pooch somewhere along the line an' there ain't no goin' back. not without a great big fight at least. but everybody's too settled, too stuck in their ways for that. all clamorin' around in their greed. bargain basement thinkin's what it is, ramblin' on about how they shouldn't care 'bout others because no one cares 'bout them.

i'd like to hope i'm wrong for my gran' daughter's sake. she's a beaut, you should see her. me, i'm almost done with it anyhow. but yeah, maybe i'm wrong. wouldn't that be the day? the day you wake up an' look out your window and everyone's thoughtful an' considerate? that day would be the day we could change things. i don't think it's likely, but i still got my hopes up.

in the meantime, my boy, i just strive. such a good word that is, strive, an' nobody uses it enough. see, most people get all fascinated with perfection. then they grow up an' realize they ain't perfect, their job ain't perfect, the world ain't perfect, their parents ain't perfect, their girl or guy ain't perfect, nothin' an' nobody is perfect, 'ceptin maybe the sky. an' so they give up.

that's what i see when i look around, lots of people who just plum gave up. but we gotta remember to strive anyway—that yeah, perfection ain't gonna happen but that don't mean we shouldn't reach for it. that yeah, maybe we're gonna be hypocrites some days and screw up other days, but we just gotta keep tryin' anyway. maybe in strivin' we'll find a sort of accidental perfection, you know, a more real perfection, an attainable perfection.

later, he drops me off at a motel in some nameless town. as we part, i look into his eyes and we say our goodbyes many times before he finally drives off.

i'm in my apartment, doing nothing in particular, looking out my window at the darkening sky. it's day, but the clouds are advancing, dark and pregnant.

a woman passes by my window. i only get the barest glimpse of her but my gut wrenches with a sort of awkward recognition. i don't know who she is but i feel as if i do. i've dreamt about her. i have to catch up to her, i have to talk to her. i'm not dressed to go out so i'm scurrying to get clothes on.

i've never had this reaction to anyone, never outside of my dreams. so i can't let her get away. i hope i don't come off as a madman, running after her, stopping her on the street trying to explain myself, but i have no other choice. so i'm out the door, dressed haphazardly, still barefoot. i'm leaping down the steps three or four at a time, banging into the walls as i round the corners. i slam into the front door. when i get it open she's standing right there, her hand up as if about to knock.

and she's smiling. it's like she recognized me and felt the same undeniable urge i did. we have shy, knowing grins, children sharing a happy secret. her eyes are the color of a marble i lost when i was five. i reach out, bravely taking her hand. she responds in kind, grasping my other hand, stepping backwards, pulling me with her. our movements have the determination and careless elegance of two lovers pulling each other into bed. it's so right. everything is so damn right. the clouds above are ready to burst.

we're in the street, dancing in the middle of an intersection as if this was our only night. we're singing, so happy together. and the bombs begin to fall, breaking through the clouds, thousands of them all around, filling the air with their dry metallic whine. we're spinning each other in roving circles, faces pulled back in centrifugal glee, heads upturned as they come down around us. we're watching the end of the world in slow motion.

and as the bombs hit the ground they become rain, erupting, covering us in their fine mist.

i'm in her arms, her presence her touch her smell intoxicating me. her face is pressed against mine, cheek to cheek, bodies intertwined among the sheets. i massage the back of her neck, my fingers losing themselves as they course through her hair. my other hand explores her back, the smooth warmth of her skin. i am this absolute love for her, a bottomless well that managed to fill to overflowing.

but something's wrong. bliss blends with despair, everything is as it should be except nothing is as it is. i don't want to think about it, i try not to think of anything, to exist only here and now. i want the universe to crack and time to halt. i forget to breathe, only realizing the suffocation at the last possible second, pulling in air with an audible gasp. the oxygen only serves as fuel. i'm going to explode. i feel it in my chest, my stomach, my mind. because i know

i'm dreaming. we were outside, i remember, i'm sure of it. we weren't lying here together. this isn't real. i'm cursed to wake, i feel it approaching like doomsday.

i close my eyes and the mechanics of the universe make themselves apparent to me. at first there is only darkness, but a darkness full of the warmth she presses against me. shapes begin to emerge, invisible yet true. gears and abstract angles, infinite in their complexity, power beyond comprehension. a glitch, perhaps a dying god's last joke, has aimed the machine in on itself. because at the very center of it all, the gears grind into each other. all this, the grand machine, the whole of the universe, the framework of existence, sits subject to this futile war.

and i focus, bind my will to the gears, hoping beyond all hope i can destroy this ridiculous machine, bring it down in on itself, force a fucking cataclysm. but instead

152

i'm ground into pulp as the universe blinks out and i'm left staring into her eyes, locked in the perfect union of unrequited lovers. i'm complete if only for an accidental moment.

i wake with a start. no. not again. i'm already trying to remember her face, i've already forgotten. but i'm not upset. i'm calm. the hazy lucidity of the dream has given me new insight: her rarity has blessed us with something that escapes most people.

maybe i'm too focused. maybe i don't get the big picture. maybe it's this distanced approach that causes us never to take it for granted, never to fall to boredom, never to be lost, swallowed by the day to day. i get the sense that she's known this for a long time, that it's why she hides in my dreams.

but i'm not sure it should be this way. in these endless moments she gives everything meaning and in doing so takes meaning away from everything else. i know, with certainty, that if she ever let me i'd be hers forever. my fear is that she never will, that i already am, that neither of us has a choice.

but at the same time, so what if i can never have her. i still love her. a more perfect love, maybe. so what if she always has to leave, our time together scattered and incomplete yet better than if she was never there at all. we have what we have. we are what we are. and it's good.

i don't feel so alone.

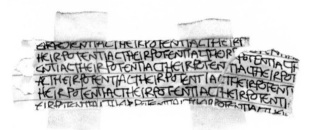

i decide i'm going home. there's a bus practically waiting for me at the station, i buy a ticket and i'm on it. the ride back is uneventful and gives me time to think. time to sort things out for myself.

it is always now, and now is all i know. sometimes i recognize this. sometimes i don't. i am nothing but the collision of memories and dreams, a cycle of forgetting, past and future.

a fly lands on my shoulder, then hops over to the window and then back to my arm. i lift my other arm to swat it and stop in my tracks. i examine it's wings instead, their fine detail. and off it goes.

i must create the most perfect self possible. i must nurture myself. reincarnation is misleading—it's not about my next life, but the moment this moment leads into, my future self, my tomorrow self.

everything is starting to make sense.

i am discontent with the repercussions of my own power, because it means that individuals who are without this power have only the illusion of choice. my reality supersedes theirs. i am not ok with this. i deny the temptation to power. i am not like *them*. even were they willing to invite me into their circles, i would not have it.

i want to teach, not rule.

because i know a secret. everyone is capable of this, of controlling the now. i can see it in all eyes, just below the surface, it's just that most aren't aware of their ability and are not reaching their full potential. everyone just needs some sort of jolt to wake them up, to evolve. just like me.

is it too much to hold people to the promise of their potential?

in their greed the others with my ability have split up the world between themselves. they revel in their power and therefore have a vested interest in keeping others powerless. power is meaningless if enough people share in it.

so they work to create and maintain this broken world in a concerted effort to keep everyone else from evolving. they bind through creating a world which blinds.

and once they create the landscape, everyone else lends a helping hand. with the world so fucked up, most people throw their hands in the air and give in to it. in abstaining from their ability, from their responsibility, they have given away the reins of control and sit subject to the will of the others already powerful.

they unwittingly spread the lies of the oppressors, further reinforcing this skewed 'reality.' their pessimistic passivity pollutes the collective consciousness and helps to build the conceptual cage for everyone else—one based on fear, distrust, futility and distraction. it feeds back into itself, creating a grand spell keeping the majority in a recursive nightmare, keeping the world what it is.

fuck that. it's a lie. we can do better than this.

i want to remove those in power by empowering everyone, by creating a landscape, an environment, in which everyone is induced to evolve. give everyone full jurisdiction over their own reality. teach them. let them wake. end the reign of cynicism, fear, and distraction so that every last human can see the now and join us in it.

the world will be beautiful when we all learn to come together in harmony rather than letting the power hungry few feast on our energy. the collective consciousness will drink in this beauty like a desert in rain and become it, blossoming exponentially until our full potential is realized. we will create another sky together as one.

i'm off the bus and back on the streets. the city air feels fresh and new even if it is polluted. the sounds are as i remember them. i feel really good. in a way, i wish i could walk home forever.

but they knew i was coming. as i turn the corner, he's standing there. he's so close he's practically on top of me.

it's definitely him. no question about it, i'd know him anywhere. my sketch is dead on, a second hand james dean. he's wearing a brown plaid button down shirt, sleeves rolled up, nice gray pants and black work boots. it takes me half a second to register that he's not disappearing into the background as always. he's there, as real as everything else. he's staring right back at me. i feel myself tighten up as it sinks in that he came for me, assassin.

and as our eyes meet, we're at war. we're looping, we're deciding the now, we're deciding who lives and who dies.

he's got a distinct advantage—i can feel my guts ripping open as he shoves a knife into me. but for once, i want to live. so i tear into the moment and try to fix it, avert it, but the loop feels strange and full with the two of us both working it simultaneously, pushing, pulling, defining.

i'm losing. there aren't very many good ways for this to go down. he caught me by surprise, and the duration of the loop is short so there isn't much to alter. every iteration is nearly identical. it feels rehearsed, we're playing our parts, following the script. thousands of deaths, and i'm feeling them all, everything ends in my blood.

he planned this, he knew exactly what he was doing, exactly how to eliminate one of his own. he's already rejoicing the kill. even if i manage to somehow survive this moment, there's the next and then the next. all i can do is prevent the click, damn us both to live forever in this. but he's stronger than that, i can tell. he's eventually going to make this happen whether i want it to or not.

and we're endless until something changes. i'm no longer where i used to be, i'm before. i'm turning the corner and i find myself thinking, it's definitely him. no question about it, i'd know him anywhere, my sketch is dead on. and then his knife is gutting me. i'm turning the corner and i find myself thinking, it's definitely him. no question about it, i'd know him anywhere, my sketch is dead on. and then his knife is gutting me. and then i'm walking, i'm approaching the corner, i'm rounding it and i find myself thinking,

this is new. this is different. the loop is expanding. and when our eyes meet now, i see surprise. i see fear. because he's still stabbing me, but i'm no longer there. i've got room to move, i've got time on my side. i'm all alone in this new, larger loop, it's no longer thick with his will. i've left him stranded in the original loop, orphaned in an impossible moment that i'll never let happen. he's inside of me.

i grab into the past. now that i've got a handle on what's happening, i can use it. i continue changing the scope, changing the scale. i'm ten feet away from the corner, again and again. twenty feet. more. i'm watching everything fade into the distance. if i keep going with this, i'm certain i could rip him out of his mother's womb. but i don't need to go that far back. i feel the loop i want and i make it click.

and now i'm sprinting towards the future i already know, each step predetermined. i can feel myself fulfilling my chosen destiny, almost but not quite reliving it from the outside. as i round the corner, there's the screeching of a car out of control, and what's done is done. thirty feet beyond where i was supposed to die, he's on the ground broken and twisted with his unseeing eyes drenched in carnage and bloodshed, lost to the now.

i'm falling victim to my own preconceptions of the world they've created. this must change. i too, must continue to strive without end.

there's something i have to do. i feel like i could head off armageddon. i feel like maybe i'll have to.

i no longer care if they find me. i will unleash myself upon them if they do. it's not that i've reached my breaking point—if anything i'm feeling calm and peaceful—it's that i don't give a shit anymore. let them come. i will show them what i am capable of, i will bring the now crashing down on them, unforgiving, i will give no quarter, i will leave nothing in my wake. fuck 'em if they can't take a joke.

i am beautiful. i am deadly. i am pure.

for once, i know who i am. i will not question myself, i will not bow down to the weaker me. i am fixed because i will not be broken. i will be my potential. i will no longer deny my inner self—i will embrace the demon within without displacing the angel. i will let myself be whole. i will overcome all odds and ascend to my place in this world. i will be generous to those in need, treasure those in love, never forgive the selfish.

i will evolve past those who attempt to maintain their horrific representation of reality to the detriment of all. i will push the limits of time and space, render them meaningless. i will rise up to bring those in power down and in doing so bring everyone else up with me. and should i become too powerful i will deny it no matter the cost. i will not become as them.

i will strive.

it's criminal almost, the way my mind plays tricks on me. it's always a step ahead, always on that next thought just a second before i'm ready for it... that meaning of life i just discovered, lost, escaping my grasp because i'm too busy with the realization that the thought was beautiful to actually remember the thought itself. not this time. i will not forget, i will carry my oath deep inside me.

movement catches my eye. ants are clumped together on the sidewalk in an arrangement that reminds me of something alien: three living crop circles, each appearing to be about a thumbnail deep. it's strange, there doesn't seem to be any food, they aren't working.

i crouch down and observe them. time passes. and now, a queen emerges through the divide between concrete plates, her wings reflecting the sun through moon. and then another, and another. three queens, three circles. the colony is celebrating the birthing of new colonies.

i dust each circle with some crumbs of food from my bag. gifts of goodwill in exchange for allowing me to witness such a momentous occasion.

i'm drawn into a tattoo shop in front of me. the interior is calming, grounded in earthen minimalism. a man is sitting cross legged inside, sketching in his book. he's on a thick rug surrounded by pillows. he looks up at me, his eyes sky blue with wisps of white clouds surrounded by a dark green ring.

we fall into looping, but there is no conflict. we find peace in each other's harmonious loops. we deflect and deny the negative, we see only hope and joy and happiness in each other, variation after variation. this is how it should be. and then, we smile. there is a shift in time, and so i begin to speak.

i need to document something, a vow i've made to myself. he halts my speech with a smile. they're beautiful, aren't they? he flips over his sketchbook so that i can see it. he'd been sketching the ants; his design flows with life. we are in total alignment. he stands, and motions me to follow him into the back of the shop. i sit down in the chair he motions at, as he prepares his ink and tattoo gun. it doesn't hurt nearly as much as i thought it would.

the subway greets me like an old friend and takes me home. as i enter my apartment building, i'm struck by a vision:

162

the door crisscrossed with yellow police tape, the inside of my apartment in disarray. it's been searched, everything tossed everywhere, books are all over the floor. her corpse found, her memory frozen in white chalk and dried blood... and the gun, gone.

i close my eyes and when i open them again i know it didn't happen. they never found their way to my apartment. the gun will be there, because it isn't not there. she will still be there.

and i'm right. i can smell her from the hallway; it's a good thing my apartment is on the top floor. it's worse when i open the door, the kept air sweet and sick with decomposition.

the bedroom door is open and i approach it with dread and trepidation. i know exactly what i'm going to see yet i still can't prepare myself for it. the thing lying sprawled across the bed is barely her. it's black and bloated, crawling with insects. fat and chewed and eaten, its skin looks soft. i could push through it with my fingers.

i hang tight against the wall, keeping as far away from her as i can. i can't break my stare; i know it's impossible, but i half expect her corpse to rise, leap across the room, eat into me, swallow my soul. the imagery only intensifies as i round the side of the bed and can see the sour remains of her face. her eyes are gone, she's staring at me with empty sockets.

when i'm at the night table, i fumble through the drawer, my eyes still locked on her face. there's a small box of ammo, nothing else. a second of confusion before i remember she's still gripping it tight in her hand.

taking the gun from her hand is an exercise in revulsion. i feel the flesh and muscle of her decrepit fingers ripping and shedding as i pry her grip open, tender rancid meat falling off the bone. her trigger finger breaks off with a wet cracking sound and falls to the ground.

i head to the bathroom, closing the bedroom door behind me. i try not to think about what i just saw and did. i wash my hands, wipe down the gun with a damp washcloth.

i go back into the living room and sit on the floor, breathing deep. it takes a long time to load the gun.

as i enter my apartment building, i'm struck by a vision:

the door crisscrossed with yellow police tape, the inside of my apartment in disarray. it's been searched, everything tossed everywhere, books are all over the floor. her corpse found, her memory frozen in white chalk and dried blood... and the gun, gone.

i close my eyes and when i open them again i know it didn't happen.

164

and i'm right. the bedroom door is open and i approach it with dread and trepidation. i know exactly what i'm going to see yet i still can't prepare myself for it. she's lying sprawled across the bed, naked, her chest rising and falling in a light sleep.

i hang tight against the wall, keeping as far away from her as i can. i can't break my stare; it's strange seeing her this way. i don't want to wake her.

when i'm at the night table, i fumble through the drawer, my eyes still locked on her face. i take out the gun and the small box of ammo next to it.

i go back into the living room and sit on the floor, breathing deep. it takes a long time to load the gun.

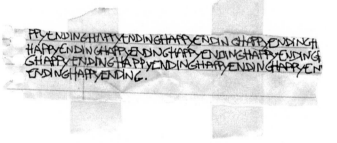

i'd give this a happy ending if i could. and i can, so i will. sort of.

i don't have all the answers. i'm not even sure i have any. i just know that something needs to be done. anything. somebody needs to set the world on fire while everyone's asleep, and it might as well be me. a new start, a new blank slate. we might still fuck it up, but that's not my concern.

nobody can promise the future but everyone can change the now. and that's our sole responsibility—change what we know is wrong without getting so caught up in the potential ramifications of change. we don't need solutions, we need evolution. now.

i have the gun pressed against my forehead, eyes closed, and i'm counting sixes again. but this time they're gentle, a soft breeze. meditation. i'm pushing the loop further and further back, further and further out. i am everywhere and nowhere. i can see through the sixes, i can see through time.

i've finally found my words and they're falling apart and coming together, connecting and rebirthing neural (neu:ral / new:all) connections long asleep. my inner voice sounds alien (al:i:en / all:i:am) but it's anything but; my new words are wholly mine. in trusting (tru:sting / true:singing) them, i can finally trust myself. thinking in this way invokes concepts more pure than any structured language could.

my thoughts have intention and direction. just as i am careful (c:are:ful / see:all:in:full) in what i say, i must be careful in what i see. careful in intention.

my eyes feel different. it's not just that i can see more. they feel hot as if there were two small suns emanating from my skull. before, i thought of eyes as being receptive, complete in taking in their surroundings. but i've come to realize (real:ize / real:eyes) they project as well as see (prophesy). the world will be beautiful (be:au:ti:ful / be:all:of:its:fullness) when everyone learns to project as well as see (proper:see).

my mind spins in its revolution (r:evolve(ution) /
r:evolve(solution) / r:evolve:soul:u:tion) / re-evolve the
soul you have shunned). i am something new. i feel it. i
think it. i am it. i'm the phoenix (phoen:i:x / full:i:exist)
rising from the ashes (ra:singing:as:he:is).

i am living lucidly (lu:cid:ly / you:should:be), i feel now
coursing through my veins. i spin worlds around the
sleeping, my vision is my spell (spell words to create
worlds : spell worlds to create words).

i'm correcting all the errors, working my way backwards.
effect begets cause, and i ripple through history
(his:story / myth:story). i right wrongs and slay their
demons, prevent them from ever existing. i'm taking
it all back. i'm creating a world (spelling:words) where
everything went right, nothing went wrong. where
everything makes sense.

i'm rushing backwards. i'm at my birth (be:earth) and
i keep going. i am before myself, further, i am beyond
myself, further. i am now, past, and future. i'm the all, i'm
breathing it in and remaking it. dismantling the grand
machine so i can rebuild it. i am creation, i am finality. i
collapse the universe into a single point of time and space
and then let it unfold itself into my design. everything's
now, but different.

when i open my eyes, i know there will finally be a world i
can exist in. and as i'm pulling the trigger, as i have it all
just right, i hear the click, harsh and loud and true.

Breinigsville, PA USA
10 November 2010
249062BV00001B/208/P